If Walls Could Talk:

The Mystery of Alton Rose

Sarah Mae Phipps

Kristen Franey, Your Compass Within Publishing

To the wonderful human to whom I pledged to tell your story; and to my dearest family and friends.

Those of you whom I have personally told about this book, I want to thank each of you from the bottom of my heart. God has used your encouraging words and your love to propel me to this wonderful moment. Your prayers and your belief in me have allowed me to overcome intense hurdles I never dreamed I would endure. Enjoy!
God's richest blessings to you all.

All my love,

Sarah Mae Phipps

Chapter 1

"Only mystery makes us live. Only mystery." – Federico Garcia Lorca

What a spectacular morning! I notice today's sunrise has painted an exceptionally glorious picture in the sky... and, there is a nice cool breeze! My goodness, it's all I can do to resist the urge to pull over just to sit and capture the moment, but I must keep driving!

I continue to enjoy the perfect sunny drive right down Alton Rose's picturesque main street with its shops, and stores, all of them unique and individual. There is of course: a coffee shop, bakery, café, hardware store, and book store. My new home: Alton Rose, a wonderful little community that still has "old- world" charm and where life moves a little slower. My quote about mystery is so good it's just begging to be put on the town's brochure, I think smiling. I am feeling a rush of excitement this morning! This is to be my first "real" day at my new job, and I am looking forward to working with Mona and the rest of my colleagues.

My mind wanders back to what's playing on the radio... Each of us has our own perception of reality and what our life within that reality should look like. Now, whether that perception of reality is right or wrong shouldn't matter. What should matter is how we take that reality and live our lives! Mother Teresa once said, "Yesterday is gone. Tomorrow has not yet come. We only have today. Let us begin."

Yes, I'm ready! I pull my car into a parking space, turn off the radio, and just sit there taking in the amazing view in front of me. I know if I have any doubts, nervousness, or hesitations about my new job at Sunny Real Estate, Mona, my new friend and colleague, will put any or all of them to rest.

Mona is our office's smartly dressed receptionist. She can always be found in elegant, professional, business attire, with a pair of pumps or heels to match. It seems she would look more at home in a high–rise office building in New York than in this cute town. I have been told there are two ways in which she wears her thick, shiny, healthy black hair: either down with long thick waves framing her face and with not a single strand out of place, or up on top of her head in a perfectly neat bun, with three good-sized curls hanging down. If it's up, she will always wear her glasses instead of contacts, and those days are usually in the middle of the week, signaling an all-business and no play kind of day. My new boss told me that Mona is as "dependable as the sun coming up each morning!" I do hope so.

However, for me, having only been in town three days, I actually feel like I've known Mona my whole life. Truthfully, she does have that vibe, and it feels so nice to count her as my first friend here. One of these days I'll ask her why she's chosen to be an office receptionist instead of an investment banker. She received honors in her degree in finance, after all. Yet, not knowing her story or where she's been, it's not really fair of me to even think negative thoughts of her. We never know the length and breadth of someone's story, nor what the person has gone through when we dare to actually look into their eyes.

I glance over and see a guy sitting across the street looking in my direction...I force myself to ponder Mona's interesting career choice... If I stop and think about it for a few minutes, I can sort of see where these two seemingly opposing jobs can, in fact, come together to form a killer job. What I can't figure out, though, is why Mona is staying here in Alton Rose, when countless opportunities in her desired field are in abundance elsewhere?

Enough pondering. *Geez, why is that guy across the street staring at me?* I get out of my car and head up the sidewalk toward our building, wondering if Mona's boyfriend had something to do with her not choosing not to pursue her real dream? *Let's see… What was her boyfriend's name? Mona had told me…oh yes, London.* She told me that he had been hired a few years back as Alton Rose's Chief Investigative Officer working for the police department, and although he isn't an actual officer, he often works hand in hand with them, occasionally even accompanying them on patrol.

Much to my chagrin, Mona had not given me any specifics when I peppered her with questions. She simply said that London never talks much about what he actually does, and told her he really couldn't say much. If this is in fact true, not only does his name suit him, but his job does that, as well as defines his character. Mona spoke of this the other day, and how much people's names and their meanings are important to her, and then ended up lovingly talking about her London again. How handsome he is, how brave and strong he is, how the name London has two meanings that seem to be consistent when you delve deeper: "fortress of the moon" and "fierce ruler of the world." That's thought to be derived from the Celtic element "lond" which means "wild or bold." According to Mona, London sure lives up to his name. I listened to Mona courteously. She is in fact a new friend, and good thing too, because with some of the crazy names people are bestowing upon their kids these days, we could have ended up in a lively debate! I still chuckle when I think of how Mona ended that conversation by saying, "Get London with me and soon he's a big teddy bear." Well, that's for her to know. I have enjoyed their warm, welcoming, hospitality, and it sure makes me feel better knowing I have a few friendly people I can trust.

I walk up to the double glass doors of Sunny Real Estate and take in the sight. I love our office building tucked in between picturesque shops. Mona has made it look so up–to–date and inviting, mixing industrial with modern and tucking in old world charm. Oh, I just love it! Still in my dreamy trance, and awkwardly balancing my coffee, I reach for the door handle, and am suddenly lurched back to reality, as one of the glass doors flies open and a stately woman very rudely breezes by. So jolting is the encounter, some of my coffee sloshes out onto the ground and I drop my laptop! *Thank God it's in a hard case to prevent breakage.* The rude woman gives no hello or good day, no apology – just vanishes!

I try to regain my composure as I walk into the common area. I glance over at Mona, our dependable office receptionist who needs an upgraded title...the poor dear looks like she's seen a ghost!

"Can someone PLEASE tell me what on earth is going on around here?" I blurt out my question rather bluntly, but this has been the third time in two days that this lady has come into our office with this mysterious fanfare. The first two were during my training. Each time she drops a note on my desk – I'll bet this time with no contact information - freaks Mona out, and then leaves! Then, like clockwork for the next hour, everyone in the office is silent and for the rest of the day no one will answer any of my questions relating to this classy-looking intruder! This time, I am sure, will be no different.

Now, I absolutely love reading a good mystery novel; I just didn't think I'd ever live in one! *This is beginning to feel like a true forget-everything-going-on-in-real-life-and-figure-it-out mystery.* A good Sherlock Holmes mystery. I giggle to myself, slightly entertained. Heaven knows I am going to have another partial day spent in silence, so I might as well make the best of it and keep myself entertained by trying to figure out the meaning of these weird notes.

Sitting down at my desk, I begin analyzing the cryptic note the mysterious woman left on my desk. I pick up the two she'd left previously, and hear Mona laugh nervously. I look over at her and ask, "Mona, how did that lady know which desk was mine? Did you tell her or show her?"

Still looking like she'd seen a ghost, she looks at me and shakes her head. "No, Megan, I never told her. I actually offered to take the note from her and told her I would give it to you when you came in, but she insisted she leave it on your desk. That's why I looked like I'd seen a ghost when you came in! She went straight to your desk, ceremoniously set the note down, and then left!"

I glance toward the doors, half-fearing the offender might reappear this time, just to throw us off.

Mona continues, "I don't know how she knew. Every desk looks pretty much the same, and you have nothing on your desk that would give a clue to anyone that the desk is yours. Goodness, you just officially started today!"

She paused, looks around, and then begins speaking so quietly I am forced to get up and go stand by her desk. "Megan, this lady is the town's legend. People say she can't be trusted. She's either hiding what she knows or she's hiding... *something*! She was involved in an unsolved crime years ago. I'm sorry, Megan, but no one in town acknowledges this lady's presence, no one speaks to her. We all simply... just... tolerate her."

I shake my head in disbelief, thinking, *Wow, this town just keeps getting better and better.* "Well, Mona, the game's afoot!" I say in my best manly Sherlock Holmes accent. "Wait a minute. Why would someone take this much time to painstakingly type short notes on cards like this when she could have handwritten them?" Mona and I shrug.

"Megan, what foot games are you talking about?"

"Really Mona, are you serious? Did you ever read Sherlock Holmes in English Literature class?"

She nods and then starts laughing at her embarrassing question.

"Mona, that is actually what I am referring to. I happen to love a thrilling mystery novel, Sherlock Holmes is my favorite. I was just being silly. I'm also a firm believer in giving everyone a chance to be heard... Speaking of being heard, would you please get me our mystery lady's contact information? I think I'm going to head over to the library this morning and do some research for a while."

Sweet Mona looks perplexed and worried but begins looking up the information. I'm not needed back at the office until after lunchtime, so I figure I may as well let my desk at the office remain anonymous and go see what I can dig up on this mysterious woman.

I walk back over to my desk to study the three notes I'd received. No name. Darn. I was hoping for at least her name or even signature. *Who does that?* I laugh as I answer my own question... *She does.* Why am I asking so many questions I can't answer... and why *does* all this matter? I turn around and sit down at my desk, taking a deep cleansing breath. I lay the three notes out, side by side, and reread them...

Note #1: Welcome to Alton Rose!

Note #2: I have chosen you to sell my estate.

Note #3: Please meet me at Oswald's Coffee Shop tomorrow promptly at 7:07 a.m.!

The mystery lady seems to be very direct, and I choose to ignore the other thoughts going through my head because I have vowed to always give everyone a chance to be heard. *In this lady's case, is it a chance to prove herself? But why did she choose me? Why can't I say no to this job? Why 7:07 a.m., why not 7:00 a.m.?* I roll my eyes. Here come my questions again.

After what seems like an eternity, Mona comes back over to my desk. Slyly sliding a piece of paper under my computer keyboard, she whispers: "Megan, anything I give you *will* be on paper. From now on, whenever you have a question pertaining to our mystery lady, you will write it down and slip it under my computer keyboard. You'll then find your answers under your keyboard the following morning. If you come into work and don't find anything under your keyboard..." Mona counts off on her fingers. "Number one, do NOT look at me. Number two, do NOT ask me about it and number three, after this moment, we do NOT have conversations about this conversation."

Mona looks around again, takes a breath, and finishes. "It simply means I've not gotten the answer you're looking for nor had the opportunity to answer it yet. Memorize all the information I give you as best as you can, and then burn the notes! Make sure it is one hundred percent... no traces of paper...burnt completely to ashes. Do you understand?"

She says all this with such conviction, even now, as she whispers, I am moved to only nod my head. She looks at me trying to find more words, but for some reason, I want to laugh and ask if this is a joke and she's humoring me by pretending to be my sidekick Watson.

However, when Mona speaks again, I know she is dead serious.

"Megan, I've lived here my whole life, and trust me when I say, there has been some crazy... stuff happen. The town's walls have eyes and ears. Unexplained things have happened that no one has answers for! Be alert. Stay focused. Be yourself, and do only what you have to, so you can sell this lady's house. But I'm warning you...this lady is tied to much more than you can ever imagine! I want to live a good, happy and peaceful life as I'm sure you do. So, if I were you, I would *not* choose this as your first thing to do here in Alton Rose."

I feel goosebumps, the hairs on my arms stand up, and chills go down my spine. "Good heavens, Mona! What on earth does everyone think this lady did?" I ask it rather loudly, forgetting in my excitement to whisper.

Mona rolls her eyes, leans down, and whispers, "Did you

comprehend anything I asked you to do and not do? Do I look like a detective or a police investigator?"

"I'm sorry," I whisper.

Mona walks back to her seat with great pomp and circumstance. As she sits down, she looks at me and winks. I think she's just given me a clue. She sure has. I deftly remove the piece of paper from under my computer keyboard, collect my three notes, purse, coffee, and briefcase and stand to leave. If I hurry, I can have a full three hours to research both the town and our mystery lady at the library before I'm due back to the office. As I wave goodbye to Mona, I wish her a pleasant morning and tell her I'll be back for my one o'clock appointment.

At that moment, the rest of our crew walks in. *Wait, what time is it?* Wow, all that happened in 14 minutes? Thankfully no one had heard us, or had they? Mona said the walls have eyes and ears. *Okay Megan, pull yourself together. Make Sherlock Holmes proud!* I get in my car and head toward the beautiful Alton Rose Library.

It doesn't take long, just a short drive down Main Street for two blocks, and then a right-hand turn onto a side street with the library. The building is a stunning sight. It has weathered the course of time extremely well considering how old it was. The library features tall, stately, round marble pillars and huge floor-to-ceiling windows that let in the warm sunlight from many angles. I look over my right shoulder and see the most unique seating in the small library garden – the benches had been made to look like stacks of books. How clever! It looks as if a very talented artist had made seating out of recycled plastic by stacking and layering it, forming it into antique-looking library books. They were even meticulously painted. Instead of heading straight into the library, I make my way over to the garden, choose a "book bench," and sit down. It is surprisingly comfortable. I close my eyes for a moment, breathing in the sweet aroma coming from the flowers. I suddenly feel like I'm not alone. Opening my eyes,

I glance around trying to find the person just as my phone vibrates, signaling a message.

As I briskly make my way over to the library steps, I give myself a pep talk. *I shouldn't apply for a library card just yet because that could be traceable by this mystery woman if, in fact, she is hiding something. I should walk in with the confidence that broadcasts I know where I'm going. I should be extremely calm and vigilant, quick, yet unhurried.* I swing the thick dark oak library door open like I mean business. I boldly enter onto the shiny hardwood floors with confidence like I have Sherlock Holmes and the entire Alton Rose police department right behind me!

I smile at a few library patrons while wondering where the security cameras are. It must be obvious to the town that I'm new to the community, and it has to be just as obvious I was hired to sell houses. So, since everyone in this small town probably knows all of this, gathering books on houses and a few others from the historical section won't seem odd.

There were two things drama class taught me in junior high and high school: make your audience believe you and become the character you are portraying.

So, let the show begin!

I make an abrupt right and turn down the row of books I'm hoping won't let me down. What luck, no one is in my aisle! I begin my careful search for… well… any book to jump out at me. I pull a few books that pique my interest, turn a few pages, glance at the sleeve of the book, pretending to ponder, then put one book back. I find two books I'm particularly eager to dive into. I seem to score in each section I browse through. I find a cozy spot near the archive section in the far back of the library, to analyze all my finds. I am so eager about all I have found, that I decide to set an alarm on my phone to vibrate, signaling me to put everything back before leaving. I don't want to be late for my one o'clock meeting back at Sunny Real Estatewith my new client.

I stack my books in piles of like subjects while glancing

around. *Hmm, there's a gentleman three aisles over who seems to be keeping a watchful eye on me, or is it just me and my imagination?* I sit with the feeling for a minute and I soon don't feel right. I pull my phone out and text Mona: *Please text me in 20 minutes!*

As soon as the man sees my phone, he disappears. I send the text to Mona anyway, and set the alarm on my phone. Then, with laptop out, and coffee in hand, I begin investigating. What was it that Mona had said? Oh yes... "Be alert. Stay focused. Be yourself, and do only what you have to, so you can sell this lady's house."

Who knew you needed this much research to make a sale in this town?

Chapter 2

If we could peel back the wallpaper of time, what would we see? What would we find?

For the next few hours, I surrender myself to thousands of pages: picture books, history books, art books, and books holding archives of the town. The last of my time is spent diving into Alton Rose's newspaper collection. I take notes, stuffing my brain full of useful and juicy tidbits, police reports, town happenings, births, marriages, deaths...I flip through pages, take notes, then turn back again, recognizing a problem. *Why are random years of marriages and deaths missing? Why are random months missing from the newspaper collection? Of course I need the very pages that are missing!*

I formulate a plan in my head regarding what's missing, and what I need copies of. Getting copies would be cause for questions from the librarian since I am not yet a regular patron... I need to think. My time at the library is drawing to a close, and I still don't know how much longer good fortune will be on my side and how long I will have this space to myself, but I really need to get those missing pages.

I begin stacking the books I am no longer using. I glance at some of the book bindings then casually over at the bookshelves, making it appear as if I'm figuring out where to return them. I am, to a degree, but truthfully I'm more interested in scoping out the area to make sure no one is hiding among the shelves looking at me. My instincts and heightened awareness are at their max, so if anything is off or I'm being watched, I will definitely know. Good fortune is still in my favor. I move some books with the other hand, while I simultaneously get my cell phone, ready the camera, turn off the flash, and silence the phone. I take a deep breath, say a prayer, and quickly take pictures of what I need.

Just as my phone slides into my work tote and a couple more books have been stacked, one of the librarians rounds the corner! "Are you finding everything you need, ma'am?"

"Oh yes, thank you," I answer in a more excited tone than I had intended. I smile and meet her eyes, showing her the utmost calm. Nevertheless, in that one instant, my entire being knows I am not to trust this woman. And I don't know why. She meets my gaze and smiles, making no effort to continue on down the row. She just stands there.

I arch an eyebrow and firmly challenge her. "Is there a problem? Was I doing anything wrong?"

She makes no effort to move or speak. *Odd. I want to ignore her, but I also want this to be over with,* so I continue. "I'm Megan, the new realtor hired over at Sunny Real Estate. I'm new to Alton Rose, not that it matters, but I just love history and was enjoying the thrill of meeting your town through these beautiful books I found." Smiling, I direct my hand over to the table where I still have a large stack of books and continue, "I was just getting ready to return the books to their shelves, if that's alright with you…I'm sorry, I didn't catch your name?"

To my relief, her stare softens a little and she manages a polite response. "Oh, you're fine, Megan. My name is Anita. Welcome to Alton Rose, it's so nice to meet you. Do come to the library any time!" And, just like that, she turns and exits down the main aisle!

I make quick order of putting all the books back while leaving one out on purpose - Alton Rose's census record. Earlier when I had looked through the countless census records, they had left me baffled. *Marriages! That's it!* That has got to be one of our missing keys. However, in order to figure this all out, I need to find the rest of the marriages, but how can I possibly locate them if they are missing? That, dear Watson, is what I must figure out. Maybe I can ask the priest if the church has records?

I simply loathe asking so many questions that go unanswered. How can I talk the town priest into letting me see those archives without raising any suspicion? I knew I would be handling this research myself. I knew I would be going at this alone. I knew I would need to channel my inner Sherlock Holmes, but after the unexpected encounter with Anita in the library, I need a moment to regroup. My phone alarm buzzes. Okay, back to the office. Time is going to be my biggest challenge, second to the wedding dates and names missing out of Alton Rose's records. I would save that investigation for later.

I triple-check my area to make sure I've not forgotten anything. Quadruple checking to make sure I have my cell phone, I quietly exit the beautiful library and head back to the office. Still, I had a longing… an unexplainable feeling of desire…to go back to the library and stay there longer. It was so warm, peaceful, majestic, inviting, and elegant. Even if you aren't immersed in a book, it would be a lovely spot just to sit alone with your thoughts. I had learned so much during my research time at the library: the history of the town and its people, how long some had stayed, and why some had left. I even unraveled stories of the town's industry and businesses, the ebb and flow of life.

Her family turned this into a respectable thriving town, but with the good there seemed to come the bad, too. After the railway was put in, much of the town's success was rerouted to make use of the train, and the river travel began a slow and steady decline. It also seems there were a few prominent men in the community who had something to do with this unfortunate demise. *But why?* Even now, centuries later and no matter the town's previous struggle, it looks like both the river and railroad are doing well. The town's river had made for an excellent escape route for criminals and thieves, but there were far more positive stories than bad. I studied and looked through countless photos of houses, aerial maps, zoning deeds, and town newspapers. There were a few aerial maps that had caught my eye, newspaper clippings on stories that I took notes on, and census listings that I either tried to remember or wrote down. All in all, even for Sherlock Holmes, it had been quite a productive morning.

Back at the office, I meet with my one o'clock appointment. Afterward, I sit back and turn my attention back over to my morning findings. Never in my twenty-five years as a realtor had I encountered such a house…or such a client! She was a lady of sophisticated mystery.

Over the course of the next several weeks, wherever I go, I sneak in a question or two about my mysterious lady, appropriately and without being obvious, of course. As I'd learned at the library, she and her family had done so much for Alton Rose and its people over the past century. Yet, there was hardly a person in Alton Rose who, if asked, wouldn't give me their opinion on the dear soul. Sadly though, no matter who I did ask, they all seemed to tell the same melancholy story of her being widowed, estranged from her creepy first husband, always looking over her shoulder, and living alone instead of being locked up "for a crime she had to have committed!" If I straight out asked someone if they'd ever met Mrs. Beauregard, they would quickly reply, "No!" And, if I followed that up by asking if they knew with one hundred percent certainty she had in fact committed the crime, they would hesitantly answer in hushed tones, "Well, no, can't say that I can."

Mona and London told me there was a group of retired guys who sit in Oswald's Coffee Shop every Monday and Friday afternoons to reminisce and talk. So, I made it my mission to befriend them. It took a few Mondays and Fridays of me coming in, ordering my coffee, walking by their booth while flashing them my award-winning smile, and sitting in the booth behind them sipping my coffee and just listening. Finally, the long-awaited day came when I was invited over to sit in on one doozy of a conversation for the next couple of hours, garnering a wealth of information from them!

A couple of the guys were curious about me and my story, so I answered as many questions as they could ask, hoping at some point it could be my turn to inquire and I could feel that they could trust me. A man calling himself Mr. Saul looked over at me and winked. Then with a charming southern drawl, gave me an all-knowing grin while inquiring, "Miss Megan, surely there must be some questions about Alton Rose circlin' inside that pretty little head of yours?"

I smile. "Actually, Mr. Saul, yes, there are! As you all know, I'm the new realtor in town, and am always looking for a little story or two to put with the houses I'm trying to sell. The newest project given to me is the selling of the Beauregard Estate. I was wondering what you gentlemen can tell me about it?"

Boy, does it get quiet, quick! A somber hush falls over our table. One guy motions for the barista, while Mr. Saul takes a long sip of his coffee. Another named Gabe stares into his steaming large mug as if the answer he is looking for will suddenly appear within the dark liquid. I smile to myself and wait patiently. As coffee cups are refilled, I check on a few clients via texts, send a message to Mona, then sit back and wait. Finally, Gabe looks up with a serious look, proceeding to do most of the talking for the next two hours, as if it would be the last story he'd ever tell.

"Back in the day, I was Alton Rose's Chief of Police," he starts, before telling us about the two fateful calls that came one Tuesday morning as he was arriving at his office. Two calls that would haunt him forever.

First, he answered a call about a young student in Alton Rose High School, who had gone to the Friday night football game with the cheerleading squad. She was last seen walking in the direction of her home after the game, still wearing her cheerleader's uniform, but she never arrived home. Thinking she'd gone with her best friend back to her house for the weekend, her family had woken up and gone about their Saturday, as usual, assuming they would see her Sunday morning at Mass, as would usually happen after most of the big home games. Yet, Sunday morning came and she didn't show.

When they asked her best friend where she was, the friend said she'd given her a hug and watched her walk out of the parking lot towards home. Naturally, the girl's parents filed a missing person's report. Gabe and most of the team spent that entire week canvassing the town, working on the case, interviewing, and visiting locations.

At the mention of this, the other two men nodded in solemn agreement. *I guess they'd been there too.*

Tired and feeling forlorn, they'd returned to the police station to accept lunch the sisters of Saint Mary's Cathedral had prepared and brought over. During lunch, he'd received the second phone call. A car had gone missing. Gabe soon realized he was talking to Mrs. Beauregard. She and her husband Luther, who was mayor at the time, had three vehicles they called *his*, *hers*, and the *going-out* car. She'd called in to report their going-out car had been stolen. Not wanting to waste precious time, he'd made quick work of the Beauregards' paperwork, then hurried back out to help the search team. Gabe said everyone in town had cooperated above and beyond what was actually necessary that day and through the following weeks as they searched for her.

Realizing it has suddenly gone quiet around me in the cafe, I turn my concentration from Gabe and look around at the three other guys sitting in the booth with us. All of them are teary-eyed and listening, reliving those days all over again. *Poor guys. This missing child affected the entire town.* The guys are so committed and focused, they each had let their coffee go cold.

Gabe takes a drink of his coffee and an amused smirk appears to one side of his face as he takes in the faces of his buddies. He takes a deep breath and continues his story, telling us about the conversation he remembered having when Mrs. Beauregard had said she'd last seen the car, and when she'd last ridden in it. Gabe sits up a little straighter when he begins talking about interviewing protocol, proper questioning techniques of suspects in question, and how to interview the witnesses.

I continue listening, just as mesmerized as the guys in the booth with me, mentally taking notes, quietly sending texts to Mona, but being as discrete about it as possible. I loved every part of this story. As quickly as he began, he suddenly gets quiet, his face becomes somber, and for a split second, the guys and I all think he is finished telling his story.

"Aw! C'mon man, don't leave us hanging!" exclaims Saul.

"Dude, not coo..."

Our eyes follow Saul's gaze as he stopped mid-word and looked straight at the coffee shop door. I don't know what is happening, but Gabe's face suddenly shifts to a look of protection and authority, lips tightly pressed together, and he sits up even straighter! Taking his cue, I go into Realtor Mode, pulling out the pictures of the houses for sale to help our motley crew not look so weird.

"So, what can you gentlemen tell me about these houses I'll be selling?" I ask, acting as if we had simply been chit-chatting.

Thankfully the guys get the hint and all begin chiming in with their opinions about each of the houses. But Gabe is not deterred. While two of the guys debate over the year one of the houses was built, I sit back and consider the eerie feeling I'd gotten when Gabe stopped talking just because a man had walked in.

Here is a Sherlock moment and I mustn't ignore it! In tune with my feelings, I now study the man. Something looks familiar about him... maybe it's his coat? As he gets his coffee and heads to the door, I realize where I've seen him! He's the guy from the bench across the street, and the same guy I'd seen in the library! I whip my head back to the guys and their conversation so

Library Guy doesn't notice me. I want to stay incognito. The guys seem to have come to an agreement on the year the house was built and are now telling me about how many families have lived in each one of the houses. *This is great information to have.*

Through it all, Gabe never wavers from his policeman's steely stare. It sends shivers up my spine. As soon as the coffee shop door closes and Library Guy is out of sight, Gabe looks at me with an intense gaze and commands, "Megan, don't you ever talk to that man without me or another officer present! Do I make myself clear?" He asks with police authority in his voice.

"Gabe, isn't that a bit extreme? I mean, what if I bump into him accidentally or…"

"Megan!" Gabe says again, "I. Am. Serious! Yes, I don't know you well. Yes, you are a grown woman. Yes, you don't know me. Yes, yes, yes, but you don't know *him*!"

"Yes sir!" I answer meekly, but with all the respect and honor I can muster out of my shaky voice. *I get the feeling he is concerned for my safety. Swallowing my pride, I realize he's got that concerned-protective-father look.* I lean in over my coffee, staring him in the eyes until a smirk crosses his face. "Gabe," I ask, "can you please tell me why?"

Gabe's buddies had snapped back to attention. Gabe smiles again and cunningly continues the Beauregard story right where he'd left off, but not answering my question. Ru*de.*

I listen intently, and then he winks at me. "Megan, this now brings me to the answer you're looking for, but I've never been able to prove… I think the guy we just saw is the reason the Beauregard's car was missing and never found. He is Mrs. Beauregard's first husband, and he was always fo…"

"Whoa, hold on, Gabe!" I interrupt, in a state of shock. The second the words come out of my mouth, I have a feeling Gabe is done storytelling for the day. It's amazing how a person can sense things when they allow themselves to do so.

Gabe looks at his watch. "Well, boys, I need to head over to my kickboxing class at the gym. Are you coming with me, Saul?"

"You betcha, my man!"

Gabe looks back at me and says, "We'll meet again: same time, same place next week for some more of the story, as long as I'm able."

I don't understand Gabe's statement at the end, *as long as I'm able.* As I walk back over to the office, I vow to not only figure out what Gabe meant but also to figure out who the mysterious Library Guy is before my next coffee-shop date with the guys. *If he is, in fact, Mrs. Beauregard's first husband, what does he want?* I think back through what I can remember. *Didn't someone say her ex had come back into town? If so, why was he making her life a living hell? What mystery was there, that no police crime-solving unit has ever been able to crack? How could it be that everyone hates Mrs. Beauregard and not her ex-husband? Why is Mrs. Beauregard's existence shrouded in mystery? How is it that I have so many questions and no real answers?* I have endless leads that lead to more leads.

Remembering that Sherlock Holmes always caught a break in his mysteries, just when all hope would seem lost, I straighten my shoulders. No worries. *I am confident Mona will help me.* As I head back to the office for the last few hours, I remember I'll be meeting Mrs. Beauregard at Oswald's Coffee in the morning, and I should be extra prepared, looking professional and well-rested. I must go to sleep early and hope my racing mind will slow down before I hit the bed.

Chapter 3

"By wisdom, a house is built, and through understanding,
it is established; through knowledge, its rooms are filled
with rare and beautiful treasures." Proverbs 24:3-4

At exactly 7:00 a.m. I have a perfectly picturesque coffee in hand – mmm, the aromatic coffee smells divine! The kind of picturesque coffee, where the mug fits perfectly in my hand, and it's the correct temperature, with the precise amount of frothed milk on top. The finishing touch is a perfectly formed heart poured in the swirled shades of caramel and butterscotch foam.

I sit down at a table in the corner of Oswald's Coffee and wait for my mystery lady to arrive. During my library search, I'd scored quite an array of pictures of her, thanks to her second husband being mayor of Alton Rose for so many years. Even though the pictures were outdated, I was able to form a picture of her in my mind, so I had some idea of who I was looking for, combined with a vague idea of what she currently looks like, having stormed past me at the office.

While I nervously sip my coffee, my eyes take in the charming coffee shop as I wonder which lady waiting in line at the counter I'll be meeting. I also try calming my nerves by admiring the coffee shop's modern-industrial, yet cozy atmosphere. The weathered floorboards have been stained into a checkered pattern at an angle. On the brick walls, they have neatly hung pictures and signs from days gone by, creating quite a mesmerizing gallery.

I glance down for fear someone might think I was watching them. *Why, for Pete's sake, is she taking so long? The note stated,* "*Promptly at 7:07 a.m.!*" *I look at the time on my phone, 7:15!* Now worry sets in. As I sit back in my chair, I continue to scan the cafe with curiosity. After about a minute, I see him, the same eerie guy I'd seen in the library!! Chills run down my spine and I gasp. Trying to pull myself together to appear calm, I focus on my facial expressions and reason with myself as I sip my coffee. *Just remember, Megan, you are in Alton Rose. This is the main coffee shop in town. Actually, it's the only coffee shop in town, so naturally, there is no reason to freak out. Where else would the guy go for coffee?* Nope, no luck. I instinctively know he is the reason my mystery lady is not here. I pull out my phone again and check my email, trying to keep things casual and make it appear as though everything I'm doing is on purpose. The last thing I want is to attract attention or seem obvious in any way.

After what seems like an eternity, the Library Guy leaves, and a few seconds later my mystery lady is standing in front of me. I stand up to greet her and hold out my hand. My rehearsed greeting goes by the wayside when she shakes my hand and apologizes for her abrupt exit from the office a few weeks ago. We each take our seats.

I open my mouth to speak again, just as she begins. "Thank you for coming promptly at 7:07 a.m. this morning, Megan. I apologize I couldn't get to your table on time. The new coffee shop owner doesn't know who I am yet and I've been dying to get out of my house, so I thought this would be a safe place! I really appreciate this accommodation very much!"

"Oh, it was no trouble at all, umm... I'm sorry, I haven't gotten your name."

Mrs. Beauregard smiles. It's a pleasant yet tired one and I suddenly feel a strong urge to help right her wrongs the town thinks she has done. I open my mouth, but she holds up a cautioning hand. "Oh, not here dear, please," she says in hushed tones, placing a finger to her lips. "Our town's walls have ears, you know. The minute I say my name, everyone will panic. It has happened to me before, you know."

I look at her in disbelief. "No ma'am, I'm afraid I don't. I'm so sorry, I didn't realize that's happened to you before. I am wondering why you insisted we meet here instead of at your estate, and why you are creating what seems to be more stress for yourself, not to mention that all of this seems to be oozing with secrets "

She nods, "Yes, my dear. I am so sorry you are feeling this way and that I put you in the middle of this, but trust me, you will understand everything very soon. I promise! Now, since we don't have much time left, I will tell you this and you can be on your way and I mine. Tomorrow, promptly at 3:03 p.m., please be at the front gate to my estate. I look forward to chatting with you then about the estate and I hope to put your mind at ease. Again, thank you so much for helping me, I really do appreciate it! Goodbye, dear. I look forward to seeing you tomorrow!"

She is already out the door with her coffee! *Wow, she moves fast!* I sit back in stunned silence, processing everything that just happened, and finish my coffee. After a reasonable amount of time goes by, I put my things back into my bag. It is then I notice a tiny corner of paper sticking out from under my phone. *Had I seen her put something there? No, but she* does *move quickly.* Still hesitant to trust anyone or anything around me since there seems to be a creepy guy following me, I deftly move it and my phone into my purse so no one can see, grab my bag, and head straight back to the office.

Safely inside the office, Mona and I keep ourselves busy until we are one hundred percent positive we're the only two people left in the building so we can discuss our day and our mystery lady. Finally, after what seems like eternity, the last person leaves the office. By then I can hardly contain my excitement. As soon as the door shuts, I begin blurting out everything and, of course, tell Mona about what had happened at the coffee shop. I describe everything in as much detail as I can. I hope Mona understands why; it's almost as if me telling it in this way keeps it all alive inside my mind and heart so I can remember it for later. As I describe the crazy meeting at the coffee shop, I grab my purse and pull out the small, white piece of cardstock Mrs. Beauregard had skillfully slid under my cellphone and hand it to Mona.

"Mona, do you think we should make a copy of this?"

"That's a great question, Megan. It's very clever!" She studies the paper. "You know, I have been racking my brain trying to figure out how I am to start a conversation about this lady with London."

Here she goes, counting off on her fingers again.

"First, I can't exactly begin a conversation like this just anywhere! Second, when he is off work, Megan, he's *off work*! He doesn't want to talk about work, think about work, or watch anything on TV that remotely resembles work." She rolls her eyes.

I giggle because Mona explains this with such passion and concentration, I can tell this has already presented itself to be a problem at some point in their relationship.

She continues. "And third, this case was closed years ago due to an extreme lack of evidence and the town was in an uproar over the court allowing Mrs. Beauregard to go free!"

"Mona… how do you know I'm talking about a case? What, in anything I've said, makes you think that I'm talking about a case? What are you thinking that is causing you to say that, and why? And, if there hasn't been any evidence, why does this entire town think Mrs. Beauregard should be in jail? Mona, you're starting to scare me."

When that last sentence leaves my mouth, I realize that is something I need to work on within me. My fear is that once I have shown this type of weakness to someone, they will no longer trust me, and it is then that the fear of what they think of me creeps in.

Mona turns and looks at me. "When a house is sold, the buyer has a right to know if anything has happened at the house, or if there are any ghosts, just like they want to know how old the furnace is, or the roof, and if any appliances need to be replaced. With the age of the estate and the fact it has only been owned by one family, how do you know something *didn't* happen in that house?"

"You are absolutely correct, Mona. It was silly of me to assume, given the age, the people, and the history of the house... I will look into more of that tomorrow morning." Gee, w*hat on earth happened?*

Mona looks over at me with mischief in her voice and quizzes me, "Now, what do we look under each evening before we go home, Sherlock?"

I smile at the nickname Mona has given me. Taking the laptop and the contents underneath, I skillfully slide it all into my bag. Then, I walk over to Mona and let her look at the note, that's once again typed on heavy white card stock with the signature stamped below, for the fourth time.

Please be at the gate tomorrow at precisely 3:03 p.m.! To the left of the gate, you will find a speaker box with a black button; Press that button and wait for the buzzer. I'll then ask you to state your name. Once I know it's you, I will then let you in.

Sincerely,

Mrs. Beauregard

Address: 373 Beauregard Lane

Mona and I stare at the note as if it's going to give us another clue. What bothers me (yes, I was fuming a little), is that I am being dragged into what seems to be a whole entire circus against my will! Here at Sunny Real Estate, we do have the option to decline services to a potential seller without reason. *What if I had another appointment at 3 p.m. already on the books? Her assumptions, secrets, and intrusion into my life are not helping her case any. If anything, it's beginning to annoy me. She seems to be taking advantage of me as the new person and assuming I will be at her beck and call until further notice.*

"Geez, Megan! What on earth are you so angry about; and why are you pacing back and forth?" Mona asks in an exasperated tone.

I share with Mona my reservations about going tomorrow to Mrs. Beauregard's house.

"Megan, it's time to close up, go home, and get some sleep. You need to be well-rested for tomorrow, and not to mention, look your best. This is your first big potential sale!"

Why can't I choose not to go? She's right, though. I don't have any other house to sell; this is my first one, although I have a few clients looking to buy homes. I stuff the piece of paper into my purse, turn out the lights, lock up, and we both go our separate ways.

At home, alone with my thoughts, I still can't shake off my concerns. I check my mail, pack my lunch for the next day, lay out my clothes, and straighten up. Not that I'm a messy girl, but I physically need to avoid all the questions and nerves bottled up inside of me, so I stay busy. For the next hour I do everything I can think of to avoid my thoughts: I vacuum, look through the mail, pour a bowl of cereal, eat, clean up and look over a few potential houses for another client. Only then, do I finally allow myself the energy needed to begin thinking about what started me on this whole journey in the first place.

Sunny Real Estate had offered me a great package so accepting the position was an offer I couldn't refuse. However, I must confess, before accepting the position, I entertained a few other offers in the city I lived in. When those didn't pan out because the positions had been given to someone else, I finally hopped on the computer to check Alton Rose's crime rate, population, and the town's location, but not much else. Maybe it was because I had never heard of the town before, and I knew nothing about it. Maybe, I wanted to see what I would be getting myself into should I accept Sunny Real Estate's offer and go live there. I'm sure other people check on town crime rates and stuff like that, right? On the town's main web page, it listed all the points I was questioning, which made for a quicker search than I had imagined. *At least they have nothing to hide*, and that appealed to me. The town also displayed the Old English meaning of Alton Rose on their web page: "town at the source of the river." *It makes sense geographically, seeing that's where it is, but why would a quiet town be so proud of that? No one does that anymore on their town web pages, do they?!* So eager was I for a new adventure, I had jumped at the offer without thinking any more about it.

Tiring, I glance at the clock. I need to shower and get to bed if I am going to be ready for my big day tomorrow. Soon after, all snuggled into my bed, sweet peaceful rest envelopes me, and I allow the deep sleep Mona had wished upon me.

The next afternoon comes all too soon. I had shown a couple of houses to a client earlier in the morning, and they had made an offer on one. The excitement! Mona brought me back to reality after lunch, and debriefed me on the upcoming afternoon, just like she would with all the other realtors, only this house and client are different. Mona's mood is different, too, almost somber. After going through the usual routine points, she lowers her voice, looks directly at me, and with utter seriousness, says, "A creepy thing happened to me last night. Please listen carefully, because I'm not repeating anything!"

I nod quickly.

"Last night London called, and asked if he could come over. He said he needed to talk to me. He sounded very serious, so I knew something was up. When he got to my house, he gave me a hug, grabbed my hand, and we walked through my entire house. He didn't say anything as we went around checking all the locks on the windows, pulling curtains closed, going back through and checking all the locks again, and taking pictures of a few windows and door knobs... Megan, he was *so* serious! I couldn't bring myself to ask why! We got back to my living room, and sat down. Still holding my hands, he told me about your Library Guy! He had come to the police station, asking lots of questions, and then was asking about you!" She pauses when she sees my eyes go wide in shock.

"London said the guy was trying to get information, but of what and for what reason, London didn't really know! It creeped him out, and he got mad when Library Guy mentioned he had been watching as you and I left work! Megan, the guy was somewhere watching us when we left yesterday evening! For all we know, he could have followed us for a while. Anyhow, London told Library Guy that he'd better not catch him spying on us or causing any trouble. The man verbally challenged London a little, but London could see he had hit a nerve, so he simply warned, 'Don't threaten me or you will be arrested!' London then told me that he and the rest of the crew will be patrolling like normal, but will have him and what he looks like in the forefront of their minds, even when they aren't in uniform. London wants us to be aware of everything around us, be careful what conversations we have in public, and we must never assume we are alone now, ever!" She barely pauses before continuing, "Well, Megan, go get 'em!"

"Gee thanks, Mona. If that was a pep talk, I'm now a bundle of nerves! Thank you so much!"

Mona smiles, like she's super proud of herself. I take a deep breath, push open the double doors, and make my way toward my car. What I said was meant to be sarcastic, but I'll let her think otherwise. Maybe I could be a little more alert and a little more aware of my surroundings. I notice there's an Alton Rose police car parked off to the side, just down the street. I survey the scene on Main Street, and soon I'm in my car, alone with my thoughts. I hit the lock button and start the engine. Chuckling to myself, I begin to think that my worrying isn't such a good idea after all. So, I take a few minutes and contemplate.

Why do we build houses when there are so many sitting empty, in need of some love and a family who cares? If walls within each house could talk, what stories would they tell? If we could peel back the wallpaper of time, what would we see; what would we find? Would we find happiness or sorrow; successes or a life full of ups and downs? In our everyday lives, we naturally want to show the world our best, whether with the clothes we wear, with make-up we put on or both; and, so it goes with the houses I sell. I want to show the best the house has to offer the new potential buyer, so we use paint to clean up an area or cover an old problem. We use wallpaper to accent a nook in the hallway or in a room, but are we really hiding a crack in a wall?

Deep inside the basements of our souls, the content within is always changing, whether for good or bad. If a house is built on a solid foundation it will weather the course of time quite well. Oh, sure, there will be problems and minor repairs, but nothing a little tender loving care can't take care of. Now, if cracks are fixed right away, we have nothing to hide, both we and our house will be ready for the world! However, if you leave or ignore the cracks in your basement or your soul, ignored or un-attended, it's only a matter of time before floods of sorrow and problems will come rushing in. When this happens, it is more costly and time-consuming to fix, and we spend years hiding or masking the problem because it is seemingly too overwhelming or too daunting a task. *Why must we feel the need to hide? Why can't we pay that extra money for a professional or a counselor to help us fix our problem? The parallels are uncanny.*

All of these questions are circling around in my mind as I drive down the winding country road toward the house I will be selling. As I near Beauregard Estate, I begin to regret every part of the trip. I want to drive away for fear of what I could be getting myself into. Well, now that I'm thinking about it, I actually *am* beginning to feel conflicted with this new fear of the unknown.

I come upon the last road before Beauregard Lane, my final chance to turn around and race back into town. *Why on earth do I feel this way?* I'd been taught to listen to my gut instincts or my intuitions, and yet now, here I am hesitating instead of listening to them! I take my foot off the accelerator and let the car naturally slow down. I flip on the turn signal so I can turn my car around, but... I can't bring myself to actually do it! Even as I am flooded by the torrent of thoughts and emotions coming at me from so many different angles, I still realize that I, for some reason, have been chosen. Even though no one at the office could tell me why, Mrs. Beauregard has specifically chosen the newest realtor in the community, me, to sell her very valuable estate.

The noise of a farmer's tractor jolts me back to reality and I flip my turn signal off, put my foot on the gas, and drive on following my GPS.

As I make my final left-hand turn on the flagstone drive, I catch a tiny glimpse of the stately house in between two trees. I remember the pictures of my mystery lady's home from the library. The word "house" isn't really an adequate description of this masterpiece, nor does it even do it justice! Nor did those pictures I saw at the library. This is truly a masterpiece. This French-inspired chateau is much bigger than simply a house! I need to think of a clever name for it that denotes respect. When I post this sale, and the potential buyer looks at the picture along with the home's title all at once, they should be drawn to it with a sense of awe – a sense of, *Wow, I want it now!* Chateau Beauregard has a nice ring to it! How lovely that the street is named after my mystery lady and her house. The street sign reads *Beauregard Lane.*

All too soon I reach the gate. Three minutes past three sure came around fast! Just as I'm about to press the button at precisely 3:03 in the afternoon as instructed, a seemingly gruff yet tired voice bellows: "Yes, I know who you are! PLEASE, do come in!"

Okay, that's weird! It didn't sound like the voice of Mrs. Beauregard ... *Wait, was she not by herself, like she told me she'd be? Did she come down with a cold or something? If not and she is okay, does the speaker system need fixing? Do I write that down as my first item for updating before the sale? Do they have cameras hidden everywhere and knew it was me as I drove up?*

I ignore all the questions circling in my head and drive straight towards the chateau. I continue up the lane, hoping to find a place to stop that offers a grand view of the whole place, so my picture can capture it all. But, I soon realize as I continue driving there is no such place, so I resort to snapping a few casual "this is what you see as you drive up to your chateau" pictures. Finally, the last two trees fade away in the rearview mirror, as I see the chateau in all its brilliance and glory. Chateau Beauregard looks tired, but in a charming way. I feel as if I've driven into the pages of a Sherlock Holmes novel... and ...*maybe I have?*

I park my car. To the left of me is a beautiful well-kept fountain. To my right, grand stairs lead up to the chateau. I snap a picture of the jaw-dropping three-tiered fountain, then practically run up the steps to ring the doorbell. Three loud, melodious bongs. *Three? Why only three? Why did I count them?* I quickly jot down my observations. As I wait for Mrs. Beauregard to come to the door, I look behind me and down at the steps I've just climbed. Suddenly, a weird urge comes over me. I count the steps: one... two... three... seven steps. *Seven, now that is interesting.* I glance back at the fountain. Wow, it is even more spectacular in person than the picture I'd seen at the library. There are three tiers: three water basins, with three spouts pouring water, and three angels holding the basins. I gaze out over the entrance forecourt with seven perfectly manicured trees, all precisely equal distance apart, lined up symmetrically, with immaculate, colorful flower beds beneath them. It certainly is a stunning sight, yet instead of eight trees, *seven?*

The landscape architect who designed this had deftly added a sweeping hedge of luscious, blooming pale yellow roses, designed to move your eyes towards the house. I laugh as I look at the rose hedge… surely there were more than three bushes? I shake my head and give in to my instincts, counting the windows on the front of the chateau: seven on each side of the door, three big double windows on the first level, three big double windows on the second level, and where the roof comes down, there is a dormer window on each side. The dormer window is made up of three small windows.

The world stands still for one tranquil moment, as I take in the breathtaking sight before me. I embrace my inner curiosity, letting it take over my mind as I ponder all the possibilities, the meanings and the significance behind the numbers three and seven. I find myself laughing at the thought that only I could explain this as my perfectionism taking over, but secretly I enthusiastically desire more than anything for there to be a story behind it all, if only to justify all those so-far unanswered questions.

The loud, eerie creak of the door lock being unbolted behind me jolts me back around to the house and away from the garden. This isn't Mrs. Beauregard who has opened the door, but rather a tired, white haired, stately-looking gentleman with a cane. *Who is he, I wonder? Is he Mrs. Beauregard's husband? Is he her butler? Why is he dressed like he is a butler in England? Could he perhaps be an older son or nephew of hers?* Since I had mentally prepared myself for Mrs. Beauregard, I am a bit befuddled to see the gentleman in the doorway, and I find I'm suddenly at a loss for words. All I can do is smile and look him in the eyes. The gentleman has kind, piercing, crystal blue eyes that seem to look deep into my soul. His smile is handsome and instantly settles my nerves.

"No need for formalities, Megan," he says in a gruff voice. "I'm so glad you could come! Welcome! Please, come in!"

Walking inside, I stare wide-eyed, like a child on Christmas morning, at the stunning foyer. I step onto the shiny black and white marble-tiled floor, as my eyes move up to the lower part of the walls, where thick wood paneling has been painted a matte white. My gaze continues up to where the upper walls are creamy, pastel, pale yellow. The coloring is quite calming and lovely, and I'm left speechless and eagerly anticipating the house tour. Numerous paintings fill the upper portion of the walls, each more beautiful than the last, and all arranged like you'd find in a palace's grand hall. Some artists I recognize by their paintings and some paintings I recognize by the artist. I feel as if I am actually in a palace. A grand staircase of dark wood with white treads leads up to the second floor. On the landing about half way up, there is the most beautiful stained-glass window I have ever seen!

I make a mental note to study the window in its entirety on another day. I am certain I will find some hidden meaning of some sort. The grand staircase flanks the left side of the foyer wall and curves its way upward, making quite an incredibly imposing statement. *Should I continue this number quest and count the stairs too?* I feel my mouth drop open in disbelief at the sheer grandeur and glory of just the foyer alone, and feel the need to snap myself back to reality!

Megan, I say to myself, *you need to pull yourself together! You are here strictly on business! You are to look over the estate and inform Mrs. Beauregard of the value of her home, what it will take to sell it as-is, and what it will cost to tackle any minor repairs needed first.*

Taking a deep breath, I gather my nerves and continue following the gentleman in front of me. He leads me to one of three double doors that lead off the foyer. *Why are all of these doors closed*, I wonder? I don't have to ask where they lead, because I will obviously soon find out.

Chapter 4

*"To add a library to a house is to give that house
a soul" -Marcus Tullius Cicero*

I am ushered into a regal and dignified – yet snug– library just off to the right of the foyer. This gentleman...this butler, I guess he is. He also gives me the feeling that he knows everything! He is so composed, and I wonder if knows even the thoughts that have entered my mind and gone unsaid.

His voice, now with vibrato and echo behind it, snaps me back to the present. "Megan, will you please sit here, while I go call Ms. Amelia to meet you in the library." He points to a plush chair indicating I am to sit.

"Yes sir," I say, sinking into the soft, plush, and very velvety chair. I let my eyes wander around the room as I wait for Ms. Amelia...Mrs. Beauregard... whoever. I resolve to be polite and use Ms. Amelia when I address her unless I'm told otherwise; it seems more respectful. As soon as Mrs. Beauregard's butler closes the library doors, I grab my phone and text my new information to Mona. I open my calendar app and glance at the next few days' appointments, just so I can look like I am working (which I guess technically I am) when she comes in, but also so I'm prepared and have an idea of when I'm available to return.

The library is not at all what I had envisioned it would look like, after studying the black and white photos I'd seen back at the library. I wonder if Ms. Amelia had the library remodeled recently? It looks like she has kept the vastly rich, dark, and very traditional wood paneling and trim, but chose a more modern black and white color palette. I smile as I take in the elegant whimsy of it all, old books mixed with new releases. A few had caught my eye as I walked in, harmoniously lining the shelves that span the far-left wall. Famous paintings, portraits of family and famous people such as George Washington and Abraham Lincoln, along with other works of both old and modern art had been thoughtfully curated and displayed throughout the room. Victorian furniture paired with modern lamps and throws sits atop contemporary rugs, a varied mishmash that all seem to co-exist in perfect harmony.

On the right side of the room is a cluster of three chairs near a huge marble fireplace. I am curious about the identity of the three framed pictures that sit on the mantel. This chateau in which Ms. Amelia lives looks as though it has a few mysterious stories of its own, just like Mona alluded to. At first glance, the chateau appears to be lost in time, but upon walking in, I realize the creative way Ms. Amelia has honored past and present by mixing new and old, modern and antique. I'm grateful for this alone time here in the library, everything seems to hold me more captivated than the last. *I wonder if there is meaning or significance within her groupings of timeless treasures?*

I hear shuffling in the foyer, voices in hushed tones, and the noise of the butler's cane clashing with the marble floor. After what seems like an eternity, both of the thick library doors open, and they enter. I stand, and with a smile greet Mrs. Beauregard while the man quickly closes the doors. She returns my smile, welcomes me, and I actually detect an amiable tone in her voice. I am pleasantly surprised, as I'd expected her to be rather harsh or brass. I feel that here within her own home she is more relaxed and calm, yet still carries with her a guarded side like an invisible shield. As hard as I try to put myself in Mrs. Beauregard's shoes for a brief moment, I simply cannot fathom maintaining a life in a town in which I'm shunned! Just glancing at Mrs. Amelia Beauregard, you would never assume each line and wrinkle gracing her delicate face, nor the house in which she lived, could ever indicate everything that has unfolded in her life - all the joy, sorrow, and strife. She reaches out to touch my arm and I am jolted back from my thoughts.

"Why the long face, Megan? I enjoy my life here in my home, tucked away from the cruel realities I skillfully avoid in town." *Did she just read my mind?*

"Please don't feel sorry for me. I do not see my life as a jail sentence, for I've done nothing wrong. Many years ago, I made a choice to accept what I cannot change, to not let anger or bitterness take hold of me, and to hold tight to the hope that someday the truth will come forth so I can be free!"

The biggest and most beautiful smile sweeps across her face, and her hand swoops up in one grand motion as if she is the queen getting ready to wave to her subjects. "So, dearie, we have a lot of ground to cover and not much time; are you ready to begin?"

I nod. She stands, so I do the same. She takes a deep breath and begins again. Her voice is without feeling. I get the impression she is guarding her heart, and I hope that she warms up to me, although my hopes are not high. She explains how dark the original room had been, and what she's done over the years to brighten it up. She shares her delight in mixing modern and antique pieces and the satisfaction she felt when it all came together, everything living in harmony.

I follow her over to the left side of the room as she continues explaining how she acquired each of the pieces. The entire wall, floor to ceiling, is full of books, with a real, working library ladder on rollers, suspended from thick wrought iron rails. In front of all the gorgeous books, on top of a plush rug, sits the most handsome mahogany desk I could ever imagine. She leads me behind the desk and over to a section of shelves that are not quite as full with books as the others. Her voice grows quiet, as she softly speaks of her collection and how many times she's reread her favorites. She seems to be searching for something. She stops talking, moves three books to the right, and lays a thick book containing the collection of Aesop's Fables down on its side.

Suddenly a section of the beautiful wall of bookcases parts like the Red Sea! The opening is just wide enough for one person to fit through. If Amelia had not looked over to her right, I wouldn't have seen or heard it open. It had slid open so silently, and I was very curious about what was on the other side. In my awe, I step forward to enter, but Ms. Amelia pulls me back by the crook of my elbow.

"You don't want to get caught in the middle when that door snaps shut, dearie!" Ms. Amelia exclaims, giggling at how quickly I move back. She immediately sets the book back into its upright position, and the door snaps shut! "A person could get hurt if they aren't careful!"

Ms. Amelia looks at me as her mood changes. "Megan, for now, none of what I show you or tell you is to be shared with anyone. I will explain why later." She takes a deep breath and continues, "This library is my saving grace. I know this room inside and out. It's what I consider to be my safe place, the place I can go to find my solitude, rest, and rejuvenation.

She pauses, and leans in, conspiratorially, "Don't get any ideas though, Megan. The police already know about my secret room; they found it years ago." She walks toward the far side of the room. "Come, let me show you the windows. And yes, they know about these, too! Back when they were installed, they were state of the art technology! You can see out, but no one can see in. And get this, when you open the window, it flips a switch and turns on enough voltage to shock a grown man to death!"

I lean in toward the window not knowing really what I'm looking at, yet remain cautious just in case. "Ms. Amelia, I mean, Mrs. Beauregard, what am I looking for? I simply see what looks to be a screen for your window."

"First, please call me Amelia, I hear the other so much, and it's kind of nice hearing my actual birth name. Second, when the shutters are open, the screens are in the middle of the window opening, instead of flush with the outside casing. This is so that no matter which way someone tries to escape, they won't be able to." Her voice drops to a near whisper. "The screens are actually tiny wires! When triggered, either by the window being opened or someone trying to break the screen, electrical current is automatically sent to every window, through all those tiny wires, and shocks the person trying to break in or out. One break in the circuit will trigger all the windows at the same time, so if there is an accomplice, no matter what, no matter which window, they will be caught!"

"Wow, Ms. Amelia, that is amazing! I must ask, you know, for sale purposes, what happens when the electricity is shut off or the power goes out for any reason?"

"Oh, we have them hooked up to their own generator! If the power does go out, the generator then kicks on," she replies, very proud of herself.

I notice she said we, so I make a mental note to ask about this later. She seems to have a sense of giddy, almost devilish enjoyment at the thought of what could happen to an intruder. She is proud that she and the inventor created this. *She's let her guard down a little.* I can sense she's not had a visitor in years, and is getting a buzz off the sheer excitement of showing me around. I mustn't have her distrusting me, so I continue to tuck things back in the recesses of my mind, making mental notes without asking too many questions.

Funny, I don't recall seeing the butler ever leave. I wonder where he went?

I begin by asking the usual questions a realtor needs to ask in order to sell a home. You know: ceiling height; when did the remodeling take place in this room; what are the measurements of this room; would the books stay in the library or be packed up before the showing; and when was the last electrical upgrade?

Ms. Amelia cheerfully fires back her answers. I find I am actually enjoying myself and her, for that matter. Still, I can't figure out how this lady could be capable of everything the town's people accuse her of! While my mind drifts to thinking of all the larger-than-life stories and conclusions people must have drawn, Ms. Amelia triggers the secret opening in the bookcase again so I can see inside. I'm so mesmerized, I forget to look for anything else out of the ordinary that may be of interest, let alone ask any more questions about the room.

"Since you mentioned this before, Ms. Amelia, has someone met their demise here at the estate?" There is more of a business tone in my voice, that I'm not fond of. But, I am curious and it must be asked. "I do have to list any deaths that have ever occurred, whether on the property or within the home, you know, past or present. I might as well ask now so you and I can enjoy the rest of the tour together without this lingering over our heads."

"Oh, Megan, you've no idea!" Ms. Amelia exclaims emphatically.

Okay, what does that mean? Ms. Amelia and I walk into a round, cozy sitting room, while she continues the story of how she and her second husband had worked tirelessly together to build their dream home, this home, giving me no time to pry any further.

From the smile on Ms. Amelia's face, I can tell we have come to a room she loves. She steps in and looks around as a warm smile comes over her. "In here is my secret round tower room. It is where I hide, where I listen to music, where I sleep, and where I work on projects; welcome to my room!"

I look around, studying the room like a crime scene investigator. The plush, soft, creamy beige carpet appears to be new. Hanging from the ceiling is a beautiful, antique, golden chandelier with crystals hanging from it. A gorgeous, upholstered, Queen Anne chair is cozied up to the window, and next to it is a small mahogany writing desk. Ms. Amelia goes over to what looks like an empty wall and pulls out a Murphy bed.

"Megan, do you know what this is?"

"I do indeed, Ms. Amelia," I answer chuckling. "It's a Murphy bed! And, you don't see these kinds of beds in such fine working order, if at all anymore, unless someone has one built on purpose."

A fleeting thought sweeps over Ms. Amelia's face as she goes on to tell me this room hadn't always been her "happy place." Gradually over the years she realized she was finding her healing in restoring and updating her estate.

"Megan, a house is a reflection of you and your personality. It can show a person who you are not only on the outside, but on the inside as well. We all need to have a safe place where we can retreat to every now and again, not only within our minds but also within our home. When those areas are violated, a part of you dies inside, and that part of your home now holds the awful memory." She shudders, as if a horrible memory has been brought to the forefront of her mind.

"After my husband Luther died, I let the stony exterior of our home reflect on my face: cold, lifeless, angry, and dry. For everyone who chose to believe the awful lie, I put the same stone exterior around me personally so I wouldn't - and couldn't - feel more pain. I let our home fall into disrepair in some places. There were rooms I avoided at all costs, for the memories surrounding the trauma was too great to bear. Even to this day, there are a couple of rooms I still avoid!" She pauses a moment before continuing.

"After a few years when the nightmare began to quiet down, John, who you met earlier, became much more than a butler. Oh, nothing untoward, my dear! He became a protector of sorts - of history, of truth, of myself... almost like a therapist to me. Little by little, he forced me to visit some of the rooms within my home that I didn't want to go into. It took truckloads of patience from him, and then some."

"For years I had put off repairs, but John knew better, and had taken matters into his own hands. When the roof began leaking, he had it fixed. When I refused to go into...well, John took care of that problem, too. Please know that a few rooms in the house are still almost too much for me to bear. John may have to take you to those rooms, we'll see. I also consider my giving of this tour more needed therapy of sorts. Sometimes it is easier to talk to a stranger about your problems than someone you know." She takes a deep breath and sighs it out heavily.

"Okay Megan, let me take you to the butler's pantry, then we'll head into the kitchen and on into the dining room."

I stand frozen for a split second taking in all she had said. Wow! She is a strong woman! She is clearly expressive in the way she thinks and puts thoughts together. A woman still with fears, but not shown to everyone. A woman who wants to trust, yet still cannot. A woman who has lived more in her lifetime than many could ever endure in two!

"Lead the way, Ms. Amelia," I say, moving back toward the direction we'd come, but she stops me.

"Oh no, Megan, this way. This way leads to the hallway here at the back of the house. Come on," she says winking as she opens a door.

Oh! I thought it was a closet.

Amazed, I follow behind her. As we walk down the short hall, she informs me that the tower originally belonged to John Sterling, her butler, and his wife Daisy. We arrive in the elegant and functional butler's pantry, which was shared by her and the Sterlings, because "they were practically family, and the kids called them Aunt Daisy and Uncle John."

A few feet further along, we walk into Ms. Amelia's gorgeous kitchen, and her face lights up with a smile! She begins talking about her and her three kids, the meals prepared, the

Christmas cookies baked, parties, late night talks over ice cream, and how she loved designing this room to mirror a picture she'd seen in a magazine article about a mansion somewhere in England. She can't recall exactly where, but she was so taken with the design, she replicated it as best she could. She describes in detail the joy of hunting for each item, and waiting months for her finds to be shipped from overseas. She shows me everything: the six-burner Aga cooker, the copper hood imported from France, and the built-in china cabinet which is home to her everyday dishware. She gestures toward the big windows that overlook the back lawn with a garden, patio, and flower beds so intricately woven together, creating her masterpiece. Ms. Amelia had completed the kitchen's design with a beautiful mosaic tiled floor and marble countertops.

"I'd had so much fun designing the kitchen, my late husband would joke that he'd created a monster, but a very sweet one," she says, reminiscing about a good moment. I smile watching this amazing woman slowly opening her heart up to me… almost like a rose with many petals unfurling. It takes time for a rose to bloom, and it dare not be forced! Ms. Amelia is like a rose in her own home. Slowly, with each story she tells of her residence, petal after petal of trust opens.

As soon as I finish taking a few measurements and pictures, she heads to the right side of the kitchen where a double doorway leads us into a very stately, elegant dining room with three chandeliers hung over the long dining room table. The room is done in whites, creams, golds, and dark rich mahogany. It is breathtaking! I glance over at Ms. Amelia, ready for her smiles and stories like I'd just witnessed in the kitchen, but instead, there is a somber look on her face and tears running down her cheeks.

"Ms. Amelia, please, I can come back another day if this is too much for you."

"No, child. Remember, for a person to be free, they must

face the memories, the fears, and the pain. They must overcome it all, to experience relief within their soul and move forward. I will face this. I cannot stay in the past. If I do so, it will continue being my prison!"

Suddenly, there's John! *It's a bit creepy like she'd snapped her fingers and poof, he appeared! But she never had snapped her fingers.*

"Ms. Amelia, you should sit for this room, here's a tissue," John urges.

As she moves to sit, drying her eyes, John takes up this part of the story concerning the dining room for her. *How odd – it is like they've both studied the same script.* John gives me the date of when the dining room received its fresh paint, when new electricity was installed and how old the chandeliers are. He gives me the window measurements for the entire house, letting me know all windows are exactly the same size. A shadow sweeps across his face and he begins to explain Ms. Amelia's demeanor.

"She'd been married and had three children with her first husband, Hunter, but soon her family disapproved of Hunter's constant drinking, which always led to anger and abuse of varying sorts. It became embarrassing to her and stressful for her children. When her family found out, they feared for her and the kids' safety. Finally, when she could bear it no more, she told Hunter they were through, had the divorce papers filed, and her father saw to it that he was on the next "slow boat" to Australia "for a long vacation."

John was funny with his air quotes. Giggling, I look around the room while listening to the fascinating story.

John looks over at Amelia, as he continues. "Hunter was, of course, mad and threatened revenge. But Amelia's father Garrick and her family had paid for everything and even arranged for a small studio apartment there while Hunter looked for work. The day the divorce papers were finalized, Mr. Garrick saw Hunter to the boat, then watched him board and sail away. Amelia and the kids thrived in their new peace and were so happy. It was then Amelia acquired the job of interior designer and hired me and my new bride, Daisy, to help her and the kids. Amelia became so popular that soon all of Alton Rose wanted her signature touch of elegance in their homes."

I glance over at her, as I'd not heard or seen any movement from Ms. Amelia since John had begun. Her facial expression has relaxed some, and she is nodding in agreement with all he is saying.

John continues on with Ms. Amelia's story. "In three years, news of her brilliant and affordable elegance had gotten around and she had helped the design firm she worked for expand to neighboring towns and even a few homes over in the city. This would take her away for about a week at a time. Seven days was just long enough for a day of travel there, for Ms. Amelia to oversee the project to completion, and a day of travel back. In her third year with the company, she landed a dream contract, and a year later she met her second husband, Luther Beauregard."

Ah, here's some history I hadn't found in the library!

"Ms. Amelia was a lady in every sense of the word. Very professional and proper. It worked to her advantage as well as her success, even though ladies at that time rarely traveled alone. But her father had trained her in the martial arts and that was a secret they enjoyed keeping. While it gave her confidence to travel alone, she still kept it secret because it wasn't considered proper for a lady of her social class back then. In her fourth year, she was asked to take on a specific contract, and a family meeting with the kids was called since this project needed her to be away for two weeks! The children naturally said yes, because they knew that extra money meant a special gift. Mr. Garrick, of course, did a background check on the family for whom she would be working, and my wife and I smiled thinking of how much fun it would be considering ourselves caretakers of the kids for two weeks, as we had never been favored with children of our own. With everyone's blessing, Ms. Amelia accepted the project, which would also seal her fate."

At the word "fate," sweet Ms. Amelia interrupts John, sits up straight in her chair, and informs him she will finish the story. He mumbles something about getting iced tea for us and leaves.

Ms. Amelia goes on to tell me about the beautiful living room and dining room she had refinished for the wealthy Beauregard family in the city. While there, she met their son Luther. His charm was endearing and he seemed to be unlike any other man she'd met before. She tried keeping her wits about her and kept things strictly professional. He was quick to respond to her needs and desires, quick to profess his love, quick to claim her as his, and was extremely patient with her. At the end of the two weeks, she was exhausted from holding him at bay, joyous in her successful accomplishment for the company, missing her kids, and wanting to come home.

"Truth was, Megan, I had enjoyed the constant and lavish attention from the Beauregards' son so much that I ignored some unsettling issues or red flags. So, when he asked to pick me up for a date the following Friday evening, I agreed."

Where is a manual on life when you need one?

"It was a whirlwind romance, one of which my family and close friends did not agree with, but none of us could put our finger on why. In a year's time, I married, becoming Mrs. Luther Beauregard. Everything was going well, until we settled into a new routine. It was then that little things here and there started bothering Luther." She takes a breath and looks wistful. I begin to realize there is a lot more to her story than meets the eye, and she's lived quite a life.

"Sometimes I wonder if there were signs that I missed. My intuition then wasn't as strong as it is now, and I dismissed many of the little niggly things that came up. They each seemed so insignificant at the time, but in hindsight… I do wonder how things might have been had I had a stronger sense of my intuition then."

Poor Ms. Amelia! I can only imagine the difficulty of looking back and wondering if she played a role by missing clues. And, I am even more curious about how her story unfolds.

John returns, carrying a tray of iced tea and fruit, and I notice another round of tears welling up within Ms. Amelia's eyes. Without being asked, John takes over as though he'd never left, picking up right where she'd left off.

"Megan, Luther left so many promises unkept. He had gotten so clever at hiding his true identity, I guess Luther felt he could continue living his lie and no one would figure it out. He would come home so drunk, that most of their conversations ended in arguments and Amelia in tears. After Luther would pass out, she'd sneak over to the tower to discuss it with Daisy and me. Daisy and I got really good at listening to every detail of their conversations, so if or when Amelia came to us, we were ready with our deduction of it. You see, when you combine a blackout drunk, as they are called, and a narcissist, you have a frightening combination. If the conversation ends without the victim getting hurt, they don't know up from down, what started it all, and they think it's all their fault. If the narcissist hasn't completely brainwashed their victim, the replay of conversations is necessary, so the victim isn't driven into madness. It's as if their soul is fighting for their mind to stay free of the narcissist."

I notice how proudly John stands as he shares, almost as if he truly is her protector. *Or guardian angel?*

"Mr. Garrick, Amelia's father, soon realized what was happening, and after he got involved, Luther backed off for a time. Luther later got the idea to build a house for them, and plans for this estate got underway. Amelia had always longed for one, but she soon realized what we'd all known for a while: Luther rarely ever followed through with promises. Amelia was fed up and dead set on holding him to this one. I think it was around this time that Luther could no longer hide his drinking, and that's when the late night fights began. Amelia was so successful in her job that she had been hiding money and investing some under her dad's name. For roughly five years, she watched for the perfect plot of land. This also gave Luther time to cool off. He wasn't cooling off though, he was getting himself into more trouble. Living off his inheritance after he got fired from his job, Luther managed to make Amelia believe he was still working! This went on for over 11 years! Seven years into this, Amelia and a group of ladies and sisters from the parish went berry picking. During that outing she found this plot of land on which the house stands."

"Wow! How wonderful! What a lucky day out!"

"Yes! Back in 1960, the price of this land was a song, and since both Amelia and Luther were loved within the community and their parish, naturally the sale was quick and easy. After they broke ground for the house, a sense of renewal came between Amelia and Luther, so for a few years everything in Amelia's life went smoothly. After finding a builder and other craftsmen within the community, it all came together for this up-and-coming couple in the Alton Rose community."

John stands with a tray of empty glasses and bowls and explains, "It was in this very room where Amelia held the dedication party for the house."

A frown comes to Ms. Amelia's face. "Megan, shortly before our chateau was completed, three men died during construction. They didn't die on the property; rather they sustained injuries and were taken to the hospital. They died there. Those three men are the ones whose pictures are on the mantle in the library. I'm guessing you noticed them?"

I nod and Amelia continues.

"Once our home was completed, we had everyone over for a dedication party. By we, I mean John, Daisy, Luther, myself, and my three children. We invited our priest, the sisters of the parish, the builders and their families, and the families of the three men who had died. It was the perfect spring Saturday. The kind that you enjoy cautiously, all the while your gut instinct never shaking the feeling that something is going to happen."

She shudders before continuing, "Daisy and I had gone all out for the party, and as much as I wanted to spend some time in the chapel to reflect, I had guests to attend to.."

Amelia pauses, and gives me a smile. "The chapel was designed especially for me by the sisters of our parish in gratitude to me and our friendship. I gave them free reign of this project with the builder and they surprised me on the day of the dedication."

I resolve right then, to ask Amelia about the significance of the numbers three and seven. I sit in a dining room chair as Amelia finishes this part of her story by telling me all about the meal, the dedication service, and the rose bushes out front that were planted in memory of the three builders. She then lowers her voice almost to a whisper, causing me to lean in.

"Megan, it was in this dining room, where I first caught Luther with his eye on one of the widows. This same woman eventually remarried and had two children, one of whom passed away while in high school. It was a dreadful time for our town. That widow hated me for some reason. She is the entire reason the town hates me."

Amelia dries her eyes again and stands. Heading through the dining room and out under the archway, we come into the foyer. The evening sun shines through the stained-glass window on the landing, casting a shadow over a particular part of the foyer. I notice there is a hidden door under the stairs.

"Ms. Amelia, this is so clever. What's inside?"

"It's a coat closet, Megan. If you touch the panel on the chair rail, where your left hand is, that part of the wall swings open." Sure enough, there it is! As soon as the panel opens, the light in the room automatically comes on, revealing three coats. One looks really old and stokes my curiosity, but I think I'll save my questions for some other time.

Ms. Amelia then opens an actual door beside the panel, revealing a small powder room. I take some pictures, walk around a little, then retreat to the foyer to look around again. "Ms. Amelia, how is this space round, yet within your library, kitchen, dining room, and powder room the walls are all straight?"

She smiles. "I wanted the foyer round for symmetry in keeping with the staircase. Luther didn't want round walls so there is some added framing within these walls here in the foyer, so I could have it my way, and when you go into the rooms, Luther could have it his way!"

"You are a smart woman, Ms. Amelia. How clever!"

"Megan, the building of this home was my mental escape, my therapy... my saving grace. I do hope you can understand."

And with that, I think perhaps our tour is finished for the day, but there is so much more to see. I also am getting the feeling that not only am I her realtor, but I am also now her confessor.

Chapter 5

"Be true to your work, your word, and your friend." - Henry David Thoreau

I can tell Ms. Amelia is getting physically tired. So am I to be quite honest. It has been a full emotional afternoon, yet Ms. Amelia still has a sparkle in her eye. I can only imagine what it must be like for her to walk these halls and reminisce. *Hmm, I haven't endured half of what she's gone through. But for Ms. Amelia, I get the feeling it must continue to be extremely taxing on her emotionally, mentally, and physically.*

"Ms. Amelia, if you'd like, I can come back tomorrow if it will help you."

"No. I won't hear such talk, Megan. Sit!"

She pats the seat cushion, signaling where she wants me to sit. So, here we are, in the middle of the foyer, on a semi-circular bench, looking up at the awe-inspiring chandelier. I, of course, start counting each of the lights and crystals. Ms. Amelia begins telling me everything she knows about the historic castle the glorious chandelier had come from, the sad tale of what had happened to the castle, and how she'd come to acquire the beautiful piece.

"Megan, always stay true to who you are; never let anyone change you. Always be an excellent friend, even when it's hard, and never make a promise you can't keep; for you will need the blessings that come from each at some point in your lifetime. That's from my favorite quote by Henry David Thoreau; the book is somewhere in my library. Oh, what a great poet and interesting philosopher he was! Megan, that quote has served me well over the years when things got rough. It still does for that matter. I also learned quite quickly who I could and could not trust… who I could count on in a moment of need…who my true friends were or are…and even who I could vent to."

She takes a deep breath before continuing. "I learned to lean back and observe, and even now I pay attention to who likes me for my money and who actually likes me for me. If money isn't the key factor, there is always something else, be it smarts, looks, what have you. In time, you quickly learn to accept what someone can offer you from their heart, as they are the ones who care."

Amelia glances around before looking intently and directly at me. "A person's eyes can give me a sense of calm or fear. When you meet someone, Megan, look at the person's eyes as soon as you can. Learn to listen to and trust your instincts. They are given to you for a reason, and you must never ignore them. So, dear Megan, be kind and compassionate, not only with others, but also to yourself as well; for you never know when the person who you helped or saved might return the favor when you are in need! I cannot say it enough, Megan. Learn to always pay attention to your instincts! Sit with any feelings that instantly come at you for a moment; don't ever jump right in! Instead, ask yourself, Does this feel right? If you are doubting yourself, analyzing something, or questioning it, for heaven's sake, LET IT GO! Move on, don't dwell! These lessons I have learned have served me well over the years, and they still do. But I want, as we embark on this new journey together, to pass some of my learned wisdom on to you, my dear."

I find myself feverishly taking mental notes of what Ms. Amelia has said, like it would be an unpardonable sin if I don't. *Why is she bestowing all this upon me? And what has she done to the woman who had brushed past me so rudely at the office?*

All too soon, with renewed vigor and excitement in her

voice, Ms. Amelia jumps right back into telling about the foyer and its furniture. Not wanting to forget any of the measurements or stories about the foyer, I quickly scribble it all down. No sooner do I finish than Ms. Amelia starts reciting information about each of the paintings and the stories behind them. She lovingly explains how each picture, chosen for a reason or a reminder of a celebration, keeps her connected to her father in some way, how each one is considered priceless in its own way. Despite the sentimentality of the selections, many are investments.

"I will *not* tell you which ones either," she proclaims rather flamboyantly.

That's interesting. She moves her gaze to the plush round rug in the foyer, where the mahogany table elegantly stands, displaying a vase of flowers. She gets quiet for a few minutes and closes her eyes. While I wait, wondering, I also close my eyes, realizing it's quite peaceful here. I think about Ms. Amelia and her constant fight to stay connected to her father and her family. Fighting to keep her own home. Fighting for truth and justice in saving her name. Fighting for her freedom. Fighting to maintain her sanity. Fighting against her first husband, and yet within it all, there was and still is, this joy and desire to live that surges through her veins! *She simply has to be extremely tired, sad, and lonely; who* wouldn't *be after all she's gone through?*

I wonder what I would have done if I had been put in her position. Throughout the last few hours, I have begun to understand why Ms. Amelia wanted to stay here at Chateau Beauregard. This is her home. Chateau Beauregard as I've come to call it, even with all its nightmares, has become her safe place, and if she's done nothing wrong...well, now I'm beginning to understand why she chose not to run away. *But why is she selling the place then?*

Ms. Amelia looks at me as if she's just read my thoughts. A shiver runs down my spine as she says, "Megan, very soon on our tour, you will ask me why I chose to stay here instead of trying to leave. I want you to know it's okay, and I won't be offended by any questions you may ask; rather, I welcome each of them. I have nothing to hide. It is not only a natural human response to be curious and ask questions, but one you must embrace in order for us to continue our journey together." I raise an eyebrow, and it finally seems as if all my questions and curiosity will serve me well!

"I will tell you, Megan, sometimes running would have certainly gotten me in much deeper trouble, so I chose to simply stay and face my fears head on. You also have to have a certain level of confidence within yourself to do that. There was a moment, Megan, when I realized I should leave for my safety and for my kids, but my confidence in doing so was not there. So sadly, that in turn allowed even more fear and doubt to continue building up around me, paralyzing me. I endured years of mental abuse causing me to stay and push my confidence deep down inside my soul. Once I learned how to place my confidence ahead of my fears, learned to sit with feelings and control the mind games, I was able to send him away."

She goes silent as if realizing what she has just said out loud. I realize she'd not distinguished which "him" she had referred to, but really, does it matter? I knew from what I'd heard in town that one ex is dead and the other, even though she sent him away, hides like a coward within the shadows, constantly causing her unrelenting amounts of grief and pain to this very day. *This life of ours can be so sad, harsh and confusing.* We find that some of the people we have grown to love hide behind a fake façade that eventually breaks before we finally see who they really are, realizing we've been lied to all along. Other people are simply their genuine, true, and loving selves. Others form opinions of us without ever truly knowing who we are or what internal or life struggles we are trying to overcome. Such is life with all its relational and human mysteries. *This is turning out to be a very philosophical afternoon.*

I suddenly feel the urge to open my eyes and try studying the stained–glass window on the landing. I turn to a new page in my notebook. I take note of the colors used, and of course count the panes. It seems to be a mosaic but from my vantage point I can't tell exactly what the mosaic is. Just as I begin to zone in on and study the stained–glass window, Ms. Amelia's eyes fly open, and she begins speaking in a hushed tone, almost as if her life depends on it.

"Megan, please listen carefully. I can only say this once! You must know that everything in this home is an investment or a gift to me. My whole life's savings and all that was willed to me from my family are wrapped up in everything you've seen or will see within this house; and somehow, no one is to ever know! Do you understand what I'm saying, Megan?" She looks at me with such hurried urgency, like she is trying to see inside my soul. *Did she just remember something?*

I can't shake off the shiver that runs down my spine. So confused by this new feeling, I can only nod my head, signaling to her I think I understand.

"No, I see you don't, so please follow me carefully, Megan. Every time Luther was out on a business trip – now what he was *really doing* is for another day – I would spend hurried hours studying paintings and pictures at the library. Then I would hunt for replicas of them in the local antique shops, or sometimes find the real thing being sold at an auction in one of the big cities. I was to inherit a large sum of money after both of my parents passed, but Hunter, my first husband, wanted my money so badly. He still does, actually. My father was wise and knew this. He would use some of my inheritance money to buy real paintings or rare first edition books to give to me at Christmas or my birthday. If sold now, these treasures would gross significantly more than he originally paid! So, the pictures and books in the library, the paintings everywhere within the house, are a mix of real and replicas. Every so often my parents would gift me a piece of furniture or a rare vase, purchased with their own money, so as not to raise any suspicions. I do know which pieces are replicas and which are real. All both exes wanted to do was spend money, and each was always looking out for himself. They thrived on how it made them feel to not only have money, but spend it."

"Once, Luther caused a scene so grand at my job, I had no choice but to quit before I was fired. I didn't need the money but enjoyed working, so I began volunteering at the local library. Have you been to Alton Rose's library? Did you see the book benches in the library's garden? I designed those, Megan! My idea ended up creating jobs for some gentlemen in the community, and they and their families benefit to this day from our success! See, I was always trying to find ways within the community to use my God-given gifts, talents, and creativity to help others. A few years later, Alton Rose's department store opened up, and I talked the owner into letting me "volunteer" in the furniture department! I not only brought in a ton of business for them, but ended up being secretly hired! It took an exhausting amount of time to convince the owner, and once hired I was able to keep this from Luther for many years, until that one fateful night!"

"The kids and I, along with the manager, were going along with this secret swimmingly. I'd been with the department store for about sixteen years, when I heard my ex-husband Hunter was still alive and had come back to Alton Rose! Hunter had come back to my town, Megan! Nothing..."

I can't help interrupting, "Ms. Amelia, first, those chairs over in the library garden are awesome!! Second, how and why did Luther get you fired? Third, Hunter, holy cow!"

Amelia laughs, smiles, and winks at me. "Thank you so much! Luther was, and still is, very crafty. He was a control freak, always telling me one thing one minute and a different thing the next. If I'd had money, I could leave. Both men were like this; I just lived with Luther longer, and he 'controlled' his narcissistic behavior a little better, because he was the mayor and had an image to uphold. He didn't want me to be happy, and wanted me to rely on him for everything, so that when my parents died he would be getting some of my parents' money. What both he and my first husband Hunter didn't know was that my parents' will prevented anyone I was married to from getting my money. You see, they had so much, and wanted me to be loved for who I was and not my money."

Geez. I can see how Ms. Amelia seems to be tortured. To have been married to two men like this, what a nightmare! To always feel like you could never let your guard down, to never be able to trust their motives, would certainly take its toll on the mind and soul. No wonder she comes across so steely.

"Instead of supporting my dreams, Luther was jealous of them, so he made it his mission to gradually begin taking away all that gave me joy. He didn't want me to be independent. He thrived on the thought of me needing him so he could make himself feel more of a man. Hunter had done the same thing, I was just able to catch on quicker. And, yes! Hunter is still alive today and somewhere around here, child! You must now also be extra careful yourself – look over your shoulder and always be aware of your surroundings. He could quite possibly be watching you, too!"

John coming down from upstairs causes me to jump. *How? There must be another way to get upstairs than through the foyer, because I didn't see John go up. I've been shown all of the main floor, and the secret room in the library, so surely if there were another back way upstairs, Ms. Amelia would've told me, right?* Odd little things are happening. My Sherlock Holmes brain has kicked into overdrive.

I'm pondering a clever way to ask Ms. Amelia about any other secret doors in the house when I hear her say, "John, why were you in need of being upstairs?"

As John heads to his right toward the dining room, he answers "I'm just doing a little routine cleaning."

I swear his voice sounds different. Ms. Amelia, however, seems unfazed and starts up again.

"It took Hunter a while to make it back here from Australia, but once back in town he began to cause problems, which infuriated Luther even more. Luther had somehow been elected town mayor, and he was wonderful to me during that seven-year stretch, simply because the entire town was watching him. I thoroughly enjoyed it," she said conspiratorially. "I am not going to lie. The kids did, too. So, naturally when he heard about my first husband Hunter being in town, he went into protective mode. He actually became a person I could live with again."

"No matter what we did, though, Hunter always found a way to show up at our house looking for something. It was because of this that we had the fence and gate installed. One night during a party, even though John had screened all the visitors, Hunter managed to climb into an upstairs window! How, no one knows! We think he had help. As it happened, John heard a noise upstairs, so he and Luther went up to check it out. That's when they found the first bedroom's window open! The police were called, the house was searched, but no one was found and nothing was gone. It was as if, other than a thud and an opened window, there was no trace of the break-in. I often wondered if one of the builder's widows were somehow involved with some of these 'random' break-ins. I could tell you a few other break-in stories, but in the interest of time, we're moving forward. To be sure of our safety, seven months later, I had the special screens installed in every window throughout the house. John and I knew, but no other living souls did, not even the kids and Luther."

Ms. Amelia gives me a grin as wide as the Cheshire Cat's, and I wonder how she knew Hunter had climbed in the window if no one saw him, and he'd left no clue it was him. *Did she assume? Amelia was onto something else; maybe someone at the party had let him in?*

"Megan, I'm sure you are wondering about my obsession for specific numbers? Well, if you go back and think through each of my stories and the details I've shared, I've already told you, you'll find out why I enjoy the numbers three and seven so much."

Of course, I want to know. I would also go back and look and think through her stories. *How could I not?* But I have no time to ruminate on her stories or the numbers at the moment; Ms. Amelia is continuing with her story and has gone right back to telling me all about the screens.

"The screens did prevent another break-in attempt, but after that, Hunter also made it his mission to threaten Luther and me, as well as try to find another way in. One random day, Daisy was helping me clean and found a pile of money stashed in an oriental cabinet. After inquiring about this to my father, he said he'd hidden the money for me to find on a rainy day. Daisy was the one who came up with the brilliant idea for my father to purchase paintings or furniture instead of giving me money. My father liked the idea, and from that moment on, no more money was sent, but rather other gifts of value so money would never be found. To Hunter's untrained eyes, he was and still is actually looking for papers and physical money. So, for now, he will never find it! I have even painted a few pieces of furniture with a special paint a friend invented. Should I ever have to sell them for whatever reason, I have a way to simply peel the paint off, and the stain or the original paint is left untouched!"

"Wow, Ms. Amelia! Does anyone else know of this?"

Amelia shakes her head sadly, "No, it was Daisy's idea and she took it to her grave when she passed away. I don't know all the details and idiosyncrasies yet concerning all these items and how we are going to continue to protect it all during the times you are giving tours."

I reassure Amelia that she and I will think of something. "Ms. Amelia, may I ask what happened to Daisy?"

"Oh, Megan, it was simply awful! I've never really gotten to say a proper goodbye either. I'm so grateful Daisy had ten years to enjoy 'her tower' as she lovingly called it. I think that's why I love that part of the house so much now and feel safe there. Back to answering your question, Megan... John and Daisy had been on a two-week vacation with their families. On their way back to Alton Rose, there was an accident, and Daisy never recovered from her injuries. She passed away in a hospital in Colorado."

"Oh no! I'm so sorry to hear of this," I hear myself say, while at the same moment, I am remembering the grove of trees I had seen driving onto the estate. *I wonder if that is a cemetery.* Knowing I could ask any question, I open my mouth to ask Ms. Amelia about the grove of trees. She interrupts me with a nod.

"Yes, Megan, Daisy was laid to rest there, under her favorite tree; may God rest her soul. It will be the same place, next to her, where John wishes to be laid to rest. There are also a few of the sisters from our parish who loved coming here to help me. But more on that later, Megan. They are also laid to rest there per their wishes. Each of these individuals was peaceful, Megan. Their souls are at peace with our Maker, and I have honored each of them as best I know how. I sincerely hope the person or couple who purchases this entire estate isn't creeped out about having a small cemetery on the edge of their property. Forgive me, Megan, but I do feel I must stipulate that anyone interested in purchasing Chateau Beauregard, in its entirety, must make their opinion known on how they feel about the cemetery immediately!"

I nod in agreement, even though I have no idea how a potential buyer will feel about this.

"Furthermore, should they purchase the estate, I insist on

there being a clause placed within the contract forbidding them to break up the property for development of any kind. If they are unable to handle these demands or hesitate in their answer, I will *not* honor it! I can't stress this enough. We *must not*, under any circumstances, take their sale and we would have to move on! Please, I do hope you understand, because you know how some people can be. They lie saying they will honor your wishes and then do the exact opposite, and if you don't know this yet, well then, you are about to find out!"

Chapter 6

"Things are not always as they seem; the first appearance deceives many."

- Plato, Phaedrus

We begin our ascent up the grand staircase. As I climb, I look around me. *What would Sherlock Holmes be looking for right now?* I take in the beautiful artwork hanging on the walls, feel the plush carpet beneath my feet. Ms. Amelia said that it had been lusciously padded so there wasn't an echo within the entryway. Since she is a woman of function as well as design, she wanted everything within the entryway to serve practically, as well as to be pleasing to the eye.

I giggle as Ms. Amelia tells me about "the ruined foyer" she designed for a client, with all their random runners and carpets they had strung throughout the space in a way that annoyed her to no end. Still to this day, she can't get over the owners, how they'd wanted beautiful flooring to make a statement, yet they had argued with her incessantly about covering it up with their precious carpets! She compromised with them by laying carpet on the stairs but nowhere else.

There's that feeling in me again! *What is being covered up within the walls of this house that no one found the first time? What is hidden that her first husband Hunter still hunts for?* I look over the railing as Ms. Amelia pauses, even though she doesn't seem out of breath.

The hidden doors in the foyer make sense given Ms. Amelia's desire of symmetry and love of the numbers three and seven... There are three big entrances to the three main areas on the main floor, so it would've naturally bothered her if there were two more doors that she could see. Instead, she hid them so that only three could be easily seen. It would also be quite easy for someone to slip in with a guest unnoticed and hide in either the powder room or the closet, then sneak upstairs quietly, but that is only if they know about the hidden rooms. My mind is racing trying to piece together how someone got inside and upstairs during a busy party without being noticed.

Three builders had died before the house was finished. This left the final two builders plus all the wives who must know a thing or two about the house. Ms. Amelia and John had both recalled the glances that Luther continued to give one of the widows during the dedication party. *How and why was everything tied to Ms. Amelia? What role could anyone else have played?*

We reach the landing. Ms. Amelia calls for John, but he doesn't come immediately. "That's funny, five seconds has been the longest John's ever taken to answer me from here; I wonder if he's okay? John! We're heading upstairs and I think I'm going to need your input for this part of the tour!"

I see Amelia counting and think it odd. I glance at my phone. I too am getting a little concerned due to the look on Amelia's face.

"Please, John, don't answer me on a bad number," she whispers more to herself.

I shift my gaze to the beautiful stained-glass window again to concentrate on something else, anything else. The window depicts the most beautiful yellow rose I've ever seen portrayed in glass. Naturally, I count window panes, too, and the number of petals on the rose. Sure enough, all the numbers match up with the others...three here, seven there. This particular rose looks strangely familiar, as I recollect seeing yellow roses recently. *Where have I seen another rose like this... oh yes! This rose is just like the roses found on the bushes out front.*

I jump a little when Amelia speaks.

"Megan, this rose is the flower our town is named after, and is the same rose you will find on all the bushes in every garden on our property. Aren't they beautiful?"

Again, it's like she's reading my mind!

"JOHN!"

This time when she calls his name he comes running up the stairs and reaches us in three seconds flat! *Running?* When I glance back at the clock on my phone, I can see it had taken a total of two minutes for him to come, if you count this final shout. I guess this isn't good.

"John, where on *earth* were you? This isn't like you, and you promised to be within earshot should I need your help with this tour today. I would feel safer if you wouldn't go so far away next time. Two minutes total, John. You know what numbers mean to me."

I look at John, who looks befuddled and a little different than when I'd last seen him, but I can't place why. He is slightly disheveled and looks as if he's been working in the garden... he also does not have his cane and he *ran* into the foyer... That's it! Wait! *Is his cane for looks? Good heavens, what in the world is going on?*

"John, you don't have your cane...you told me you weren't going to work in the garden... speak to me, and tell me what is going on." Ms. Amelia is quite controlled, her voice quiet and calm, but her eyes tell a different story. This must be the face she learned to put on when talking to Hunter or Luther. If this man isn't moving like John, he at least sounded like him when he answered Ms. Amelia, apologizing for the delay. *He said he had been getting some vegetables from the garden and flowers for a vase to put in her room to cheer her up. Hmm.*

I still want to know why he doesn't have his cane? It all must have been too much for Ms. Amelia because she says, "Well,

John, hurry and lock up, and please see Megan to her car."

Abruptly, our meeting ends.

We both watch John leave, and quite easily without his cane. Ms. Amelia sighs, wiping a tear from her eye. She turns to me with a hushed voice.

"I'm so sorry we can't finish our tour today. John's lack of punctuality and sudden change in personality has me quite shaken; I do hope you understand."

I nod, as she slips a note in my hand while she is speaking to me. I steady my nerves by concluding that she had the note with her all along just in case she emotionally couldn't finish the tour.

John is soon back from locking up, and Ms. Amelia and I meet him at the bottom of the stairs. I notice he now has his cane, his normal speed, and is back in his original clothes. *Wow, he certainly changed fast... but he couldn't have, considering he moves so slow!* There is nothing I can do to feel less anxious; I'm so shaken and tons of alarms are going off inside me. Nothing feels right.

John looks at us, confused. "Going so soon, Megan? Our tour isn't over yet, or is it? I'm sorry, Amelia, did I miss something?"

I really want to run! This whole encounter has me freaked out, and I'm going to be driving home in the dark as it is. I look over at Ms. Amelia making her way to where John is standing. She is more visibly shaken than me. While Ms. Amelia and John are deep in hushed conversation, I quickly text Mona explaining what has happened, and wonder if London or one of the other cops in town can keep an eye on me and my house for the evening. It's imperative I have a plan as well as someone to know when I arrive safely back home.

Mona texts right back, as if she's been waiting for me to text her.

Yes, will do! A weird guy came to the office asking about you. I don't know who he was. Gave me a creepy feeling. Didn't tell him anything. I'm taking the security tape from our office over to London when I close up. Then, unless he asks me to stay with him, I'll be going straight home!

As I glance back over to Ms. Amelia and John, my phone signals another text from Mona.

London is sending a cop to your neighborhood now! He'll text you when he's within view of your house.

I reply with a thumbs up and slip my phone into my purse. When I look up, Ms. Amelia appears calm, which is a relief. John now seems to be his normal self…well, the normal I am slightly more familiar with. I turn and head toward the door.

"So, it's all set then," Ms. Amelia says. "We'll finish our tour tomorrow; I *am* looking forward to it. Good night, Megan!" She winks, waving at me as she exits into her library, and I'll bet, over to her secret room.

I step out into the crisp evening air. The fountain lights are on. A smile spreads across my face as I take in the beautiful serene view before me. I imagine the spectacular view it must present from the front bedroom windows. The crystal clear water melodiously cascading gracefully over the three fountain tiers soothes the crisp nighttime air. The lights from the house twinkle off the water and onto the angels, with the glow casting comforting shadows across the drive and nearby hedges. As I take in the beauty, I notice there are more lights strategically placed around the house, all creating a beautiful image for a great evening photo. I graciously thank John and head down the steps towards my car. As I open my car door, I look back and wave. John waves back and promptly goes back inside. I quickly take two pictures of the chateau in the evening, one panoramic, then jump in my car.

Alone with my thoughts, I begin asking myself questions. I can't help it. *Why did Hunter return? Why were the glances between her late husband Luther and the widow so bothersome to*

*Ms. Amelia and John, even to this day? What happened to the Beau-
regard's missing car? Why does everyone think Ms. Amelia did...
well... whatever it is they think she did? Alton Rose was practically
started by her family, renowned and loved by all, so why is she hated
for something that no one can find her guilty of? Why is this all
beginning to consume my thoughts? Why do I have so many questions that remain unanswered, and geez, I'm only about half way
back into town!*

Unable to stop my questions and feelings of frustration,
I glance into my rearview mirror just in time to see a car without
its lights on, pass under a street lamp behind me! I guess I should
have been more observant as to when they began following me,
but I didn't really see the car until now. This is both strange and
so dangerous because it is dark outside and only the moon and
a few random street lamps light the way. I suddenly get the feeling that I'm not safe and need to call for help. *No, I can't.* If the
person following me has a two–way radio they'll hear the police
scanner dispatch. I voice dial Mona and thank God she answers. I
tell her roughly where I am, that I'm being followed by a car with
no lights on, I don't feel safe, and that I have quite a lot to share
with her tomorrow.

She hangs up, and within a couple of minutes the car behind me is being pulled over. I keep looking straight ahead and
driving home, even though part of me is dying to find out who
was in the car, how long they've been following me, and what my
note from Ms. Amelia says. In my hurry to get home, I haven't
even looked at it yet!

As I turn onto my street, I notice a police car slyly parked
a few houses past mine. Sweet relief. I nervously answer a call
coming through on my phone. I don't recognize the number.
My confidence comes back to me as the voice on the other end
lets me know in a hushed yet reassuring tone that he is the cop
parked down the road, that he sees my car and is ready, if needed,
to remain on the phone.

"Oh, yes! If we could stay on the line while I go inside to make sure everything is okay, I'd be really grateful."

Turning into my driveway, I hit my garage door opener as I nervously scan the area. All looks well. Once I am safely in my garage, the policeman then tells me he'll be out here awhile, so I can go to bed and not worry. I hang up with a heartfelt thank you.

Sleep will be more easily said than accomplished. Wow, I need to process all of this! Falling into the nearest chair, I take a deep breath. No sooner do I sit than I feel a strong desire to meticulously check around my bungalow, making sure all the windows and doors are locked. As I begin moving in and out of rooms checking windows and doors, I mentally prepare for morning while being very careful not to turn many lights on, so it appears I am following the officer's suggestion of going to bed. I do what I can to get ready for bed in semi darkness while inwardly I am freaking out. Having checked every single door and window in my house, my brain finally registers the feeling that I am safe.

Placing my phone on the charger that sits on my nightstand, I crawl into bed saying prayers for protection as well as prayers of thankfulness that I am safe. My adrenaline is so high, surging through me, it takes a while lying in utter darkness before my body suddenly realizes how exhausted it is. These last few minutes before I finally fall asleep, I have one last thought... *Before I go to sleep, I should get up and send the pictures to Mona.*

Chapter 7

"Be strong and courageous! Do not be afraid or discouraged. For the Lord your God is with you wherever you go." – Joshua 1:9

I wake up in a sheer panic to my phone ringing and pinging, along with sunlight streaming in my window like it is noon. I'm disoriented from the feelings that come from being suddenly jolted awake when a second earlier I had been in a deep sleep. Trying to ignore my fuzzy brain fog, I sit straight up in bed, rubbing the sleep out of my eyes as they adjust to the bright sunshine. "Oh no, I must not have set my alarm! I overslept! Oh no, I never sent Mona the pictures I took at the estate! Shoot shoot shoot! I never read Ms. Amelia's note last night! Oh geez, I'm probably late to work," I groan out loud. *Ok, Megan, pull it together! First things first!*

Completely dazed and still with a foggy brain from waking up so suddenly, I run downstairs to grab the note from my purse.

We will finish the tour tomorrow afternoon precisely at 3:03 p.m.!

Thank you,

Amelia

I glance quickly at the clock. Good, I have some time. I remember her sneaky talent; how she was able to produce this note out of thin air. Letting the note fall, and still ignoring my phone ringing and pinging with messages, I run into the kitchen and turn on the coffee maker. I may be late but I still need my coffee.

Running back to my room, I head straight to my nightstand and check my phone.

The text from Mona reads: Take your time coming into work, but please come in as soon as you can! The police have just left our office and I don't want you to be here just yet, because you know why, but I really need to talk to you. Oh yeah, our office is a mess!

Holy cow, what on earth has happened? I finally succumb to the realization that I must answer and acknowledge all the phone messages and voicemails so that everyone knows I am alive. My heart is still pounding as I sit down on the rug in the middle of my bedroom and have a few minutes with my phone. I couldn't resist this rug when I saw it, it's just so soft and fluffy, even if the white is a little less than practical. Okay, I have three calls from the police station and three voicemail messages, along with two texts from London. One says, "Get to the police station ASAP," and the other is instructing me to remain calm and mentally prepare myself to identify a man they've arrested. *Good heavens, what in my world is happening?*

Oh man, Sherlock, I'm going to need lots of coffee today! Ignoring the third message, I call the police station straight away and let them know I'm coming. In weird and cautious tones, I receive instructions as to what room I am required to go once I arrive. *I must admit I am a little thrown off by the person's sudden shift in tone when I stated my name. She was so polite and friendly when she first answered. I have no idea why she's suddenly stony and cold. It's not like I've done anything wrong!* I send a text to London letting him know I'm okay and on my way to the station. Then I ask for verification of what the stern person on the voicemail had instructed me to do. In four seconds a text comes back from London. "No. We'll be waiting for you at the front entrance. See you soon!" *Oh geez, what does that mean?* I have never been to a police station, let alone been questioned.

I finish getting ready, choosing a black pinstripe business

suit with a white button-down shirt and red pumps. Thankfully my foggy brain is now lifting, thanks to the coffee. I go through my morning checklist as I prepare to leave. My hand reaches for the door heading to the garage, as common-sense sweeps over me like never before. *Megan, sit yourself down and pull yourself together. Breathe and find your inner calm, because it won't do you any good to be scatterbrained all day.* I close my eyes, so thankful for coffee, as I let the wonderful aroma overtake my senses. I concentrate on my breathing and calm my rapidly beating heart. *Get yourself together, Megan.*

It occurs to me that if I had run out of the house frantic- ally, I would not have grabbed my coffee. I fill my thermos and car mug. *Oh, Sherlock, I'll definitely be needing it all! Can a person ever have too much coffee?* Giggling to myself, I take a few sips and text Mona, letting her know that I'm leaving the house for the police station, and after that, I'll head over to the office. Just as I'm dialing Alton Rose police station to ask a question, Mona calls.

The second I answer, she begins in a hushed yet excited tone, giving me no chance to even say hello. "You are never ever going to believe what happened last night! Girlfriend, we are in so much trouble! Megan, I think London is mad at me, and the police department thinks we did something! They want my phone, your phone... I might have to go in for questioning be- cause I forgot to replace the tape in the security cameras! Ohhh- hhhh, this is all my fault! Oh geez, our whole office is a mess, everything is a mess! Megan, it's going to take us a while before we can open our doors to the public. I'm in enough trouble, and now I remember I'm in deeper because I'm not even supposed to be talking to you, so I'm hanging up, okay? You delete the evi- dence that I called you, and I'll do the same. WAIT! NO! We better just leave it, oh geez, Megan, say something!"

"Hello, Mona." It is my best attempt at reassuring her that everything will turn out fine. "I'm about to head over to the police station. Once I'm finished, I'll come to the office. Mona, I promise, we are going to be fine."

She hangs up. There is no point in asking any questions until I get to the police station since I have nothing to hide. *Coffee, purse, phone, work bag, check.* I say a prayer for courage as I hit the garage door button. I am ready to seize the day head-on, just like Sherlock Holmes! Well, sort of, since he never had a phone or a car.

True to his word, London and another officer meet me in front of the police station and are to my car by the time it's in Park. I'm confident London is with the same officer who was watching my house last night...*at least he* looks *really tired. I'd be tired, too, after staying up all night.* I'm escorted into a grey-walled room and told to sit. London comes in and stares at me with pity in his eyes, but then instantly switches to all business. His sudden shift gives me the impression that he is having an inner monologue with himself and deciding who he will be, good cop or bad cop! *I am surprisingly calm for never having been on this side of the law before.* London wastes no time peppering me with questions, and I answer as concisely as I can. And then, the part I have been dreading...

"Megan, where were you last... No, I can't. Listen, Megan, I don't want to do this, but it is my job and I have to. Last night someone broke into your office building. It was ransacked as if someone was looking for something. The front door's glass was shattered, drawers were open, papers were scattered everywhere, and even Mona's computer was stolen... someone or some people were looking for something. Time will tell us if you or Mona are tied to the person seen in the security cameras from the business next door. Last night, your office's security cameras were turned off, which in turn disarmed the security system for your entire building. So, I ask you now, Megan, do you know who, how, and why? Please tell me what you know, and state your side."

I sit in stunned and awkward silence, my mouth open

in disbelief that any of this is even happening. The sudden fear is paralyzing, and I'm not sure where to begin, because I know nothing. I pull it together and cautiously begin, maybe telling a little more than I should, and maybe with a little too much emotion, but I desire more than anything to clear my name and Mona's.

"London, I promise you, I have no idea what happened last night at the office. Until you said something just now, I had no idea our security system was even wired to work that way in our office. You also know I couldn't have done it, because there was a cop stationed outside my house all night! While I was at Ms. Amelia's yesterday, Mona informed me via text that some creepy guy had been in our office inquiring about me, talking to Mona and most of my colleagues. No one gave him any information, but the guy had clearly upset Mona and the others. Mona said he'd seemed irritated when he left, which prompted her to do what she told me she was going to do. She informed me she was going to remove the tape and would then take it over to you after she locked the office for the night. We all clearly want to know who that was."

I try to read London's face. The best I can get is that he is irritated that his girlfriend was put in jeopardy with this whole mess.

"Mona had to have told you this, I presume, because she was dead set on having you figure out who the creepy guy on the security tape was. I also suspect no one in the office really understands exactly how the alarm system works, up until now. When I was hired I was given a briefing on how to use and arm the system. I was told two things. First, under no circumstances was ever to mess with the security panel to the right of the doorway, as it was set to automatically turn on seconds after we'd lock up for the night. Secondly, I was warned that no matter what, we leave promptly at five o'clock sharp or the alarm system would be triggered and police would be alerted."

I take a deep breath, collecting my nerves. *London knows where I was! I do feel bad for him being forced into this, trying to do exactly what he's been trained to do, and yet here he sits, having to question his girlfriend and her friend. He already knows most of the story, and yet no matter what, he must do his job.* Having steadied my nerves and the quaver in my voice, I continue with what I know.

"London, at precisely 3:03 p.m,. I was at the entrance gate of Beauregard Estate. I remained at the estate and in close company with Ms. Amelia, who never left my side, until a couple minutes before I called Mona asking her to call the cops on the car that was following me. That is how I called for help, in case the person following me was listening to the police scanner."

London jots down some notes then looks up. "Mona, please give me exact times that you remember, what you remember; tell me what all you were doing at the es…" His voice trails and with a huge sigh, he adds, "Oh yes, I'm also going to need to see your messages on your phone along with any photos you may have taken. Answer the specific questions, then sign and date it at the bottom for your file."

"FILE? London, if I am not a person of interest, why should I have a file?" *Bad things happen when you don't have a lawyer present; I watch the police shows on television! But I honestly cannot see a reason I should need one. It* has *to be obvious I could not have been involved.* I breathe in, trying to calm myself down.

London laughs, shaking his head.

I quickly remind myself that none of this is London's fault. He certainly does not need to be this kind, and he could have cited conflict of interest and given this to one of the officers I don't know. I politely take the consent paper and begin reading it thoroughly, my gut instincts reassuring me that all feels okay. I pause and pretend I'm looking over another part again while I think through what exact messages are really in my phone. Random calls and texts to home, random calls and texts to friends, calls to my mother and other family members, calls to Mona, and to the parish convent. Thankfully Mona and I hadn't said anything via texts that could possibly incriminate me or her. I look at London.

"London, I was there with John and Ms. Amelia, as she is in the beginning stages of trying to sell the estate, because it's my job. Since the house has not yet been staged and has had some repairs over the years, I naturally took only a few pictures of the outside. What do you want to know, and why do you think I did it?"

London suddenly looks uncomfortable, which I find interesting. He puts on his bad cop face. "Megan, I don't necessarily want to think you did this, but this is all standard protocol we must follow. So, you said you were with John and Ms. Amelia at Beauregard Estate from 3:03 p.m. until you called Mona about the car following you out of the Estate? Why not three o'clock?"

I am completely dumbfounded that he's wasting time talking to me and nitpicking over 3 minutes, when clearly there is someone else out there. I answer with my voice oozing with frustration that I cannot mask. "That is a question for you to ask Ms. Amelia. I honestly don't know why. Her instructions were for me to be at the estate at precisely 3:03 p.m. and press the call button, and it was precisely 3:03 p.m. when I pressed the call button on the entrance gate. Seriously, London, have you checked the tape Mona gave you? I would bet it has the picture of the thief or vandal we're looking for. Who, by the way, is probably out running around waiting for one of us to surface. He or she could be headed over to Ms. Amelia's. So, again, at precisely 3:03 p.m. yesterday, I was at Beauregard Estate until about 3 minutes before I called Mona about the car following me." I barely take a breath before continuing.

"And, no London, I can't tell you the exact time I called Mona, because I was using my car's voice-to-phone dialing so I could pay attention to my driving like a good citizen of the road.

And again, I didn't want to call 911 because if that person following me had a police scanner, my call would be on it. And yes, London, it will be exactly two minutes before Mona called you about me, so that time will also be on your own phone as well. London, you yourself originally left a voice message this morning for me, requesting that I come down to the police station to identify someone. The signing of this paper talks nothing of that, and I know that for me to identify people I do not have to sign any papers. London, I hardly know anyone in this town by name, so how can I identify anyone? Please, London, what's going on?"

Thankfully, London chuckles a little at my quick attempt at humor to lighten the mood. Truth be told, I'm still trying to stall a little bit longer because I don't want to willingly hand over my phone just yet. While I have been in this room, my phone has been giving alerts. I've missed multiple calls, a vibrating notification twice alerting me about incoming emails, and now someone else is calling! I want to have a chance to see what's been coming in before I hand it over. *Who knows what could've been sent to my phone!*

"Well yes, Megan, you will have to identify someone, but I do need you to sign these papers allowing me to see your phone. It is standard protocol to rule out suspects. This has nothing to do with the idea that you did it, but rather proving you didn't do it."

This time when he says it, I feel like something isn't right and I want to leave. Panic within me is starting to rise, mixed with anxiety because I can't get calm. Just as the door opens, I feel instantly at peace, and confidence I'd not felt before sweeps over me that I can't describe, as there stands Gabe! London stands in respect.

"Sir, with all due respect, you weren't called into this room, this is a private invest...meeting."

The peaceful feeling Gabe had brought into the room is now gone, and my inner dialogue goes crazy.

"London, you said you weren't investigating me! Now I'm confused and hurt. I've already told you that you need to look at the tape Mona gave you and ask her questions. I have already told you where I was, and it is ONE THOUSAND PERCENT OBVIOUS. I was in my house and frightened for the remainder of the night last night while a cop, who *you* deployed, sat in his car across the street and watched my house all night! If you think I managed to sneak out from the back yard, you are mistaken! There's a motion sensor light in my backyard that would've lit up the night sky and alerted the cop out front to come running! So, unless he was asleep in his car, ask him if anything happened in my backyard or if I tried to get out."

Gabe puts his strong hand on my shoulder to silence me, and I feel a familiar calming peace wash over me again. While addressing me, he matches London's gaze and speaks calmly. "Megan, I've also been interrogated, along with my coffee shop buddies, and Mona is being questioned right now, too, bless her soul. Megan, please breathe, hand over your phone, and then try identifying this man. If London will allow it, I'll explain everything to you, the questioning procedures, and how things will look moving forward"

He turns away from me. "She makes a good point, London, and technically has a solid alibi for last night after 10 p.m. So, while I understand being thorough, you are wasting valuable time as you beat around the bush. As I mentioned to the officer who interrogated me, Megan lives two doors down from me. I saw her car drive into her garage at 9:45 p.m. Why do I know the time, you ask? Well, I thought it was odd that a cop would be camped out on our street. I had let my dog out to do his business before we all went to bed. I also thought it odd that Megan was out so late, so when I saw her car pull into her driveway, I naturally glanced at my watch trying to figure out the situation because I was both concerned and curious."

Great back up!

Then, looking back at me. "Megan, if you have nothing to hide, please sign the paper and hand your phone to London so they can match yours and Mona's texts. Then, after you finish identifying the man, we'll leave."

London broke Gabe's gaze to look at me with my outstretched hand. I had signed the paper, and handed it along with my phone over to him while feeling the strong urge to speak. "You know, London, it shouldn't take you but a minute to look at my phone since I've not been in Alton Rose for very long, let alone Sunny Real Estate. Any other names you may recognize are potential clients and buyers, plus family and friends. I do need to get to work soon, so I hope this won't take much longer?" London makes no reply. He simply gets up, gives his head a nod, and is out the door.

Looking around the room hastily, Gabe rushes to sit down. He pauses, seemingly satisfied with something, and speaks quietly with a new-found intense urgency. "Megan, listen carefully, I don't know how long we have in here before they either come get you for identification or think we are talking and turn that speaker on over there." I follow Gabe's nod toward a black box hanging close to the ceiling.

"Here is what everyone in Alton Rose knows of you. You are the new realtor in town, who went yesterday to Beauregard Estate. For almost a decade Amelia has been trying to leave Alton Rose, so naturally everyone will automatically assume *that* is the reason you went out there. I want you to think through the people you have noticed the last few days before you go into that room. Next, the room you'll be going into has a thick cement wall about waist high. The rest of the wall is literally a very thick, soundproof one-way mirror. No one will be able to either see or hear you, but you will see and hear them. Men will file into the white room on the other side of the glass, each holding a number, and then the person seated at the desk will ask you a specific question. You don't need to know a name, you simply need to..." Gabe stopped when London appeared, interrupting.

"Oh, hello, you don't have to stop talking on account of me, Gabe. Please continue."

Gabe looks at me, slightly taken aback and as if trying to regain his confidence and control. "Well, Megan, once the men file into the sealed room holding a number, you will answer the person's questions with your honest answers, and hopefully one of the guys holding a number will be the intruder. It's that simple!"

I play along. "Oh, wow, is that all? I feel better already. Thank you so much for taking the time to explain the process to me. It has calmed my heart and now it doesn't seem too frightening. Thank you, Gabe."

We simultaneously look at London who seems to think we are now making light of this all. Ms. Amelia had mentioned no one in the town likes her, but she never said that those who come into contact with her would now be made into suspects or accomplices for simply being in her presence. This is absolutely ridiculous if it is in fact true. And, it makes me all the more eager to get back to her house for the rest of the story, also getting another chance to hunt for clues to clear Ms. Amelia's name.

I start to speak, but as if he knows what I am about to say, Gabe suddenly looks at me and shakes his head no, forcing me to have another inner monologue to release my ever-increasing anxiety. *I'm really floored that London, has changed so much. I'm going to try thinking positively and not read into this. I want to believe him when he says he doesn't want to think I did it, but he suddenly seems not to trust me. What a shift in just an eight-hour span! I vow to try believing he is simply doing his job, and since his girlfriend is my friend, he finds himself walking a fine line with this whole ordeal.* He is trying to remain straight-faced and show no partiality, because he doesn't want anyone else on the force to ask me questions. *Yeah, I'm just going to keep telling myself this.*

Gabe motions for me to stand and we follow London into the lineup room.

It is exactly as Gabe said it would be. He should know; he was a sergeant and then moved up to chief of police, staying in that role until his retirement. He remains at the door and gives me a reassuring smile and a wave as it closes. To my left is a stern looking woman eyeing me over the glasses that sit on the tip of her nose. She is seated at a small wooden desk with a laptop on it. To my immediate right stands London. He presses a button and says two words, "File in!"

The woman asks me to let her know if any of the men look familiar and if so, to state their number.

I turn to London. "Exactly why am I trying to identify one of these men? I mean, which issue?" There have been so many all of a sudden in just a few days!

London clears his throat. "So I can clear your name. I am simply following protocol. Megan, I believe you, and you have to find it in your heart to trust that I am not doubting you, but rather protecting you. After you left the estate, someone managed to break in there, but by the time we arrived, they had already gone. Thankfully, John was there. After he answered our questions, we dusted for fingerprints, but the only other set we found, aside from John and Amelia's, we think, was yours. We also found a smudged set that we're currently working on identifying. I will have to take your fingerprints, too. Shortly after we got back to town, the break in occurred at Sunny Real Estate. There was no tape in the security camera, so naturally that disarmed the alarm system..."

"Oh geez, this doesn't look good..." I interrupt with tears welling in my eyes. *Inner peace, get it together, Megan. London is on your side,* I begin telling myself as I feel my tears threatening to surface. "London, just please promise me you'll look at the tape Mona gave you."

"Megan," interrupts London, "the car that was pulled over for driving with no lights on, the guy in the tape, and the person who broke into the estate could all very well be the same person, or they both know each other. We aren't quite sure which it is, so that's why we need you, Megan."

London hands me a tissue and, once again, assures me he simply has to rule me out as a suspect, which is standard procedure. "I promise, Megan." *So far, each of my alibis have checked out, so I need to calm down and breathe. I'm safe,* I think, *for now.*

One by one, the men take turns stepping forward, and with each command, they change positions. None seem to cause a panic like I would expect to hit me when seeing them. "London, may I see them in different positions? Is it possible they can all start with their backs to me, then turn around so I can see their faces. Then, if we could have them sit?"

He looks at me funny, but obliges. The instant shift to compassion on his face compels me to explain my reasoning. "London, I'm looking to recreate the feeling of being unsafe after seeing a particular guy on a park bench, and then the same guy from behind before he turned around at the coffee shop." I must have said something right, because a huge grin sweeps over London's face.

"That's brilliant," he mutters to me, then gives the command and everyone scurries. Knowing this, and executing the plan, requires more work than I'd anticipated. I open my mouth to apologize for the sudden ruckus I've caused.

As if he's read my mind, London looks over and says, "Megan, don't even think about apologizing. The idea is truly quite clever! One of these guys just *has* to be it, and if this is what it takes, so be it! It is my job and I'm happy to oblige. I want you to know… you are being really brave. Thank you!"

Even as I thank *him* for the kind affirmation, I wait for the feeling of bravery to sweep over me… *Nope, still not feeling brave.* I pause, as a thought comes to me… *Don't we all, somewhere deep within ourselves, crave this inherent desire for excitement or something new? If we do, and we embrace it, we then find ourselves deep within the middle of it. Yet how is it that, more often than not, fear and insecurities quickly come to invade our thoughts and hold us captive? Why is it, when we find the courage to face our fears head on, doubts then cloud our path? It is within these moments, that we who are trying to be brave find ourselves longing to hear one person speak what we should already know:* I believe in you, you can do this, brave one!

I, too, want instant bravery. I wonder if this is why Sherlock Holmes had Watson. I smile to myself. There's that calm again.

Chapter 8

*"Do not forget to show hospitality to strangers, for
by doing so, some people have shown hospitality to
angels without knowing it." Hebrews 13:2*

Out of nowhere, like some divine intervention, Gabe is instantly standing beside me. "Gabe, how do you *do* that? How are you even allowed in this room?"

He smiles reassuringly. "You need a friend right about now, do you not?"

Okay, at this point I want to ask if he is actually the answer to my heart's prayer, maybe the archangel Gabriel sent by God from heaven, to help me stay calm. I regain my composure and produce a gratitude-filled smile, followed by a nod. As we stand here lost in our own thoughts and staring intently through the insanely thick glass, the final chair is brought in.

Gabe smiles. "Brilliant move on your part, Megan! I must say you were definitely thinking on your feet, which is the sign of a great detective! I was so worried you wouldn't be able to recognize the guy you needed to, and wanted to have you suggest this very thing!"

How does Gabe do it? With the uttering of one sentence, he instantly makes me feel so calm and relieved.

"I'm confident you'll recognize the guy London is after! No, wait. Please let me confidently rephrase that. I know you *WILL* recognize the guy now. Don't apologize for having the boys do this for you." He sighs. "Okay, Megan, I need to go back outside now. Remember to stay calm, tell the truth, and find your confidence. It's almost over, and then we'll be allowed to leave."

I turn to ask him the question I'd been thinking earlier, but he holds up his hand with a smile and as quickly as he came, he's out the door again.

The police are soon finished reorganizing, and it's all hands on deck. Apparently, a chair can be viewed as a weapon, so extra cops are needed to make sure there's no funny business. London and the woman return to the room I'm in, and we begin again. As guy number three sits down in his chair, I gasp, and motion to London that I think that's him. I'll be one hundred percent sure once he does the turn around. There is instant commotion outside the door, as well as Gabe giving someone a dressing down. I hear a woman's voice arguing and instantly recognize it. I lean over and whisper. "London, that voice sounds like the voice of the librarian who was eyeing me weirdly the day I went to the library. She made me feel uncomfortable, like I couldn't trust her, and I sensed she was up to no good."

London looks a little shocked by my mention of the librarian, but jots down some notes, nodding his head as I continue telling him everything. I should've been looking at the next guy walking in, but instead, I tell London everything about my research day at the library. It's like I can't stop. I feel like I need to tell him.

Whatever I've said inspires him, and he begins writing again with feverish haste. It doesn't take but a minute, and after answering a couple of London's questions, I look up and gasp. "Dear God in Heaven, are there *two* men we need to watch for?!" Shaking, I drop to my knees asking this, suddenly feeling the need to hide.

London sternly tells the guys to exit and protectively helps me to my feet. "Megan, start talking."

I comply. "London, men three and five have to be connected somehow. I've seen them both! Number five looks like... rather he reminds me of someone, but I can't place it at the mo-

IF WALLS COULD TALK

ment. I can feel it, they are both up to no good and both give me the creeps. I saw guy number three across the street, sitting on a park bench watching me one day. He's the same guy I saw eerily hanging around the day I was in the library. Now I get the feeling he was actually watching me! Guy number five gives me the same eerie feeling, and I sense fear with him, but I'm not sure yet why he looks so familiar." Then I get it. "London, he looks like Ms. Amelia's sweet butler but in old street clothes. Her butler John, by the way, is an absolute sweetheart and I certainly didn't feel unsafe in his presence, but that is impossible…isn't it?"

I suddenly doubt myself, not wanting to cause any more grief for Ms. Amelia. London has his colleagues bring guy number three and guy number five back for the "turn around" view, while the others are sent away. I feel the sudden urge to tell London all about the weird happenings in the foyer at Chateau Beauregard the night before. I tell London everything weird that I remember noticing, right down to Ms. Amelia's butler John acting in polar opposite ways within minutes. Even though I didn't feel fearful, I sensed something was off that day.

London is instantly intrigued, assuring me he will hold both men for further questioning. He sends the woman and her computer away with orders. After she is gone, London turns, giving me a wink. His voice softens and a huge grin spreads across his face.

"Sherlock, I think you might be onto something that no one's been able to figure out for almost half a century! If you think your conscience and nerves can handle it, I'm going to need you to help me do some spying while you're going about your normal job in getting the estate ready to sell for Ms. Amelia. You and Watson will have to promise me you'll do everything I say, execute how I ask you to, and not for a single moment doubt me. Do you think you can do this?"

"London, is Watson a cop?"

He bursts out laughing, as Gabe appears behind him.

"Watson is Mona. She told me about the little joke the two of you have going on, and so... Gabe, don't scare me like that! Why are you always doing that? Geez man, it's creepy enough around here without you sneaking up behind people!"

Gabe smiles. "I actually did ask if there was anything more I could do for you both, but I guess you were laughing and didn't hear me."

London and I look at each other with suspicion. Neither of us had seen nor heard Gabe come in, and when I had noticed he'd come in, he hadn't said anything, because his mouth hadn't moved. The guy has to be an angel, I reassure myself, trying to calm my nerves. I hear London telling Gabe he might have a job for him and his cafe buddies, but it will require a dart game and burgers at London's house Wednesday night. Gabe excitedly says he'll creatively get the word out and they'll see him at five on Wednesday evening. Thank God this room is soundproof. I can hardly contain my excitement at the amount of secrets now flowing freely between us all.

For the next thirty minutes we devise a plan that will include Gabe and his buddies. For various reasons, the guys will each be given random tasks to do within the upcoming days and weeks, but I won't know about any of their tasks. However, if I see them, I'll know that they are "following orders." Mona will continue reporting to London, and I have been given my communication orders. Since Gabe lives on my street, he assures me that he and his pooch will now be keeping an eye on my place. Gabe informs me that he walks his dog, Ralph, three or more times a day: early in the morning, around one in the afternoon, and at least once between 8:30 and 9 right before bed. Gabe reassures London and me that he and his dog will make sure to continue keeping their walk time in the evenings sporadic.

Suddenly Gabe's face lights up as if he's just gotten an idea. "Listen Megan, my wife and I need to go out of town this weekend. Would you like to dog sit for us?"

Before I have a chance to process and answer, London expresses his approval at the sheer brilliance of it. Gabe and his wife have an adorably fluffy, cappuccino-colored Great Pyrenees named Ralph. *The sweet dog has already met me so...* My thoughts are interrupted by Gabe telling me that he, his wife, and Ralph would be over Thursday evening to chat so Ralph can acclimate to my home, and drop him off for the weekend. They'll arrive back home Sunday evening and pick him up then.

Finally, I start feeling more relaxed and like myself again. I find it interesting how each person processes stress differently, and what it can do to someone when they least expect it. I search for my phone to glance at the time, but then realize London still has it. He's still discussing the Wednesday night plan with Gabe... but I really do have places to go and things to do. After a few more minutes, I can't handle it anymore. I simply must interrupt them.

"London, if I am finished, I really need my phone so I can head back to the office."

Nodding, London leaves to retrieve it.

Gabe speaks the second the door goes shut. "Megan, they've made copies of the pictures you took outside at the estate as you were leaving at night. There was someone hiding behind one of the trees, and that's why it's been taking so long." He chuckles, "Now, don't get spooked out. London just told me while we were devising our plan. And may I say, Megan, the pictures you took of the estate were amazing! Ms. Amelia will absolutely love them, I'm sure! Well, all but the one..."

Of course Gabe doesn't tell me which one. Maybe it's the one with the person hiding in the trees?

"Oh, and by the way, they had to enlarge the pictures, because they needed to identify who was hiding behind the tree. My guess is it's one of the two guys you identified, but time will reveal that to us. They can only hold the guy who broke into your office last night. However, they *are* getting both of their fingerprints now, thanks to that picture. I do fear both men are connected to each other in some way. Now it's simply a matter of finding out how, because neither are talking."

I nod. "Yes, I've had those same suspicions, too."

London returns wearing his million-dollar smile and hands me my phone. "Megan, you are free to go and all of the Alton Rose police department is extremely grateful for your brilliant contribution."

I stand, as relief washes over me. "I do hope I don't let you both down."

Gabe, London, and I all wink in agreement, knowing what the weekend holds for us. So, armed with my special instructions and orders, I straighten my shoulders, put a smile on my face, and confidently make my way down the hall. I feel Gabe's calming presence leave me. I still wonder if this wise, gentle, and kind-hearted man is not human, but actually an angel sent to guard over Alton Rose in some special way; or Gabe has a guardian angel leading him until all her answers can be had. Whether he is the angel or is being guided by one, his abilities, wisdom, and calmness are quite uncanny; his movements so swift and subtle; and his presence is always felt.

WHAT on God's green earth am I doing? All great heroes and heroines, when going to save the world or a person, never truly know what they are getting themselves into, and yet they never seem to be afraid. Whether in a movie, comic book, or television series, each hero and heroine are faced with fears of their own that they must conquer, and yet they somehow manage to put them aside or conquer them and go forth regardless, but, *how?* How do they do it? This is what I am wanting to tap into, because when I really stop to ponder this, the villain at some point in the battle of good versus evil brings the hero or heroine's fear to light. They are faced with their nemesis or their fears, and it always shows up, in either an obvious or subtle way right when they least expect it. It seems to happen right when everyone's guard is down and good is winning. So, not only do they have to fight or stand up to the bad guy, but they must face their own fear head on and conquer both at the same time.

Do all brave heroes and heroines train so they can conquer their fears? Or, do they simply brush their fear aside and ignore it? In many cases, in the end, they learn to use their fear to their advantage, or as a stepping stone to move forward and conquer the bad guy. *So, in the middle of it all, do they suddenly get a sickening feeling in their stomach, too?* I think I'm feeling it now, actually. I am practically ready to throw up, I'm feeling so scared!

I wish I could turn and ask Ms. Amelia this question. She is, in fact, the heroine of her own story, and seems to have mastered the art of being brave quite well, or has at least been putting on one heck of a show all these years. Me? I'm told I wear every emotion on my face and I probably couldn't lie to a bug if I needed to! *I'm not really sure if this is a good or bad thing? I question the intentions of those who say I am strong or brave, and doubt that their words are true; but why do I doubt them? I certainly don't always - if ever - feel brave. And I worry that if I* am *brave people will have higher expectations of me that I may not be able to meet. Maybe it makes us stronger? I guess it's both a blessing and a curse.* Time will, in fact, tell the extent of my bravery in this new quest I find myself pursuing.

Before I get into the car, I nonchalantly scan the area, seeing nothing that is cause for any alarm. Once safely in my car, I lock myself in, breathe deeply, and check my phone for the time and any messages I might need to address before leaving. I'm doing great on time, all things considered. Mona left me a few messages on the cleaning progress back at the office. She vented about being questioned down at the police station, and Ms. Amelia called... *Ms. Amelia called 15 times!?! What on earth for?* Panicking, I look to see if she left any messages. *Okay, she's left two, and both are incredibly cryptic.* I take another deep breath and exhale, trying to calm my pounding heart.

As I listen to each message a second time, all my fears start lining up in a very straight line, and all of my bravery vanishes. By the end of her second message, I am utterly relieved my morning had been spent in the police station, because it now gives me a chance to assure Ms. Amelia with a concrete alibi. I should be able to convince her that all the happenings at her estate were out of my control and prove to her that I, too, went through a barrage of police questioning of my own this morning.

As I start the car and drive away, I am both excited and terrified for the remainder of the week!

Chapter 9

"The secret of change is to focus all of your energy, not in fighting the old, but on building the new." –Socrates

Walking into Sunny Real Estate, I am relieved to see our beloved office area is beginning to look normal again. Not that I knew how awful the state of disarray had been this morning, but my mind had formed pictures, and judging from the excitement in Mona's voice combined with all her text messages, I can safely assume our office had looked like a hurricane hit it. What is particularly interesting are our front doors. Mona had said they'd been shattered, so I was very relieved to see new heavier glass doors had already been installed. Looking around, I see Mona has already made a few changes to our office, which actually makes the layout more appealing and efficient. After taking a moment to assess, I walk over to Mona to see what help she needs.

The second she sees me, she authoritatively puts her hands on her hips. "Oh no, you don't! Park it over at your desk and look over all your emails."

I make a sharp turn and quickly sit down at my desk as I was just told to do. She is right. I really should look at my emails, address Ms. Amelia and her fifteen phone calls, and sketch out the rest of my crazy week. Adjusting my keyboard to center it, I smile. Mona has slipped a note under my keyboard. Not knowing to what extent I am now being watched, I leave the note in its place, retrieve my phone from my bag, and begin tackling my messages and emails head-on, bringing order to my life. Through it all, I am careful to leave tomorrow completely open for Ms. Amelia.

During all of this, Ms. Amelia's two cryptic messages continue to haunt my mind. *I know I should call her, but I don't want to face her barrage of questions.* I sigh. *I have no more excuses; I simply must call her. It might be easier if I call from our office phone...* I straighten my shoulders and decide to face the music! Above all, I have to make sure Ms. Amelia is going to be okay. I'm not sure how she is going to react, and that makes me nervous that she will assume I am an enemy rather than an ally. Once I hear her voice, I can figure out how to approach her list of questions, as well as discuss finishing the tour of her home so we can get it ready to sell.

A new thought occurs to me. *I have an added nemesis... John, the butler!* I laugh, feeling as if I am now living within the game of Clue! Should I let myself trust Ms. Amelia's butler? Moving forward, talking inside her home is going to be a difficult problem to figure out. I suddenly panic, wondering how much John had heard Ms. Amelia telling me about her paintings, items throughout the home, and certain pieces of furniture when she was talking about it all in her foyer. It seems she trusts him implicitly, but... that guy in the line up today... Well, no matter what, I must call her! I can't worry any more, what happens... happens.

Just as I dial Ms. Amelia's number, she storms through our office doors! I am grateful to hear her phone ringing in her purse, knowing that she will eventually see I had indeed called her. I know from the two messages she's left me, that she is very distraught from all the happenings. Bless her. Not caring who hears her, she begins talking to me with an excited tone about how she is frightened at the thought of staying in her home since the police have arrested John, and now that he's locked up, she doesn't know if she can trust me, either; someone has messed with her security system, accusing me of...

"Wait! Stop, Ms. Amelia! Please excuse me for interrupting, but did you just say they have John in jail? I'm so confused. He practically walked out of the police station with me, after we were cleared."

Ms. Amelia starts answering me, but I can't comprehend it all. I mentally just can't process her chatter. Behind her, I see Mona standing at her desk, frantically waving her arms and pointing to her phone and then to me. I'm relaxed as I reach for my phone and look at the time. This might be an answer to my prayers and an easy way to get Ms. Amelia and me back into her house. We really need to get her tour finished before anyone gets out of jail. If John had actually been the one leaving with me, he should've been home already, but either way John and Ms. Amelia would've passed each other on the road going back to the chateau. I am sure I can figure that out later, but right now I just can't make sense of it all. I have to tune out Ms. Amelia for a moment and her endless excited chatter. It's imperative I remain calm...for both of us.

When she finally takes a breath, I ask her to please take a seat at my desk. "Ms. Amelia, I need to finish this call, and then you and I will work everything out in a calm and timely manner."

She sits. Sweet silence falls over the office.

I take my phone and walk over to the desk closest to Mona's, glancing at my phone. A few minutes before, Mona had forwarded a message from London, stating they'd arrested John. The picture of mine that they'd enhanced showed *him* hiding in the bushes!

Picking up the receiver at the desk where I'm standing, I pretend I'm talking on the phone, just in case Ms. Amelia is listening. For emphasis, I speak slightly louder than is necessary.

"Thank you so much for holding," I chirp with all the business cheerfulness I can muster. I look over at Mona as she gestures to my phone. "So what day are you wanting to tour that home?" I ask loudly, while at the same time frantically typing a message to Mona. I'm explaining that it couldn't possibly have been John in the bushes, because he was the one who had just shut the front door when I'd left. As soon as the door shut, I heard the lock click into place. I heard John with his cane begin walking away, and I immediately turned around, snapping the two pictures, before going straight to my car.

I let my pretend client on the phone know that 10 a.m. would be perfect. Pretending to add a house tour to my phone's calendar, I watch Mona read my text and go white as a sheet! I thank my imaginary customer on the phone, hang up, and head straight back to Ms. Amelia with a plan.

Sitting at my desk, I look at Ms. Amelia while planning what I'm to say. I try to read the faraway look in her eyes that is mixed with numerous emotions on her face. No doubt she is shaken up, full of fear, possibly angry, and very confused, so I must figure out which of these combinations to anticipate. Taking a deep breath, I courageously offer words of peace and assurance to her. "Ms. Amelia, I apologize for the current discombobulated atmosphere here. Last night, our office was broken into. I was unable to return your calls, because I was being questioned all morning at the police station."

Finally, after hearing all of this, her gaze softens. "Megan, it certainly appears as though you are telling me the truth, as I can see even your front doors have changed from when I was here last. I feel my intuition tells me you are, but I don't know what to believe or who to trust anymore. I no longer want to go home since John won't be there, but I know I need to, because I'm not welcome anywhere else. Do you have any time this afternoon to go with me to the chateau? We are free to talk there."

This was music to my ears. "Yes, I am free, Ms. Amelia. We can go right now, if that works with your schedule?"

"I'd like that. Let's go, Megan."

As I wait to follow Ms. Amelia home, I quickly send a group text, alerting London, Gabe, and Mona what I'm about to do and where I am headed. Letting my seat envelop me, I take a deep breath and exhale while facing the thought I don't want to think...*John could possibly have a twin brother!*

If he does have a twin, what would he or his twin want at the estate? Why was the possible twin hiding outside in the trees? Does John even know his twin is here? If John knows his twin is here, is it that John is looking for something and got his twin involved?

Now, if John doesn't know his twin is here, first, that would definitely be weird. Second, who would stoop that low? Third, does poor Ms. Amelia know any of this? Is it my place to even tell her? If I can tell her, where would I even begin?

With the quiet around me, it's as if another storm of thoughts begins erupting in my head. *Was the guy watching me from the various benches around town Ms. Amelia's ex? Why wasn't her ex husband ever locked up in the first place? Why was the librarian at the police station? How are all these darned people connected, or are they? Will I even be able to get Ms. Amelia to talk?*

Oh, there are still so many questions without answers. I text London, "Wow! Should I say anything to Ms. Amelia?" He replies almost immediately. "NO! Continue as you have been. She won't trust you with anything if she knows you know." I send a thumbs up back.

Ms. Amelia signals, pulling out of her spot, and we head toward the chateau.

I casually look around as I drive, making sure we're not being followed. The people of the town and Ms. Amelia have a lot of heart-changing and soul-searching to do if they are going to put the past behind them and move forward in peace. Metaphorically, it's exactly like driving. The windshield in the front of the car is large and clear. The rearview mirror is small, and the back window can sometimes be tinted and blocked by seats or people. The view in the rearview mirror is small for a reason; as we are driving forward, we need to safely concentrate on what lies ahead. As we drive down the highway of life, we are meant to look forward and pay attention to what is coming up.

We shouldn't get so caught up in missing and wishing for what we left behind, or longing for something we just passed, that we lose sight of what is in front of us. It's been left behind for a reason, and we must leave it there.

If we focus on the past, it hinders our change and progress; it keeps us from missing the now and the new opportunities that are waiting to be ours. That being said, we must never forget the past, because we are to learn from it and move forward as better, healthier versions of ourselves. And, it is here that I feel it will be terribly difficult for Alton Rose to forgive, process, and move forward. Most people in the town seem dead set on Ms. Amelia paying for a wrong that, reality and investigation are slowly showing us, she never committed. I cannot fathom the countless minds who have believed this lie about Ms. Amelia. If I didn't know better, I'd say it feels as if we are trying to undo a curse!

I am very grateful for this quiet drive, as it's allowing my heart and my mind to clearly begin putting order to all the chaos that has been happening so I can process it all. Heaven knows what will be coming up in the near future. I know that organizing my chaos will help tremendously. I find myself talking out loud, as I go over all that has happened, what I know, who I know, and how it all fits together. It's imperative I tread lightly on revisiting the break-in at the office earlier. I must keep a safe distance from that one, so my emotions don't get the best of me.

Yet I can't help asking myself, *what exactly was the person who broke into our office looking for?* It seems as if nothing was stolen, just everything out of place! *What was so secretive that they couldn't just boldly come in and ask? What was so important that they felt the need to destroy someone else's property?* Ugh, more questions. However, London pointed out I've been asking great questions, so I hit the record button on my phone, and list the questions again out loud. I forward the recording to London. This drive is turning out to be quite enlightening and helpful. I can only hope it has proven the same for Ms. Amelia, too.

As we pull up to the gated entrance to her grand estate, I begin sensing the heaviness, anxiety, and fear of what I think Ms. Amelia is feeling knowing John isn't at the chateau. The noonday sun shines its light on many places a person could hide around the estate, highlighting areas a person could jump into the shadows. It's as if its sunbeams are giving me clues by directing my eyes toward various areas to which a person could quickly escape. I'm grateful it's only noon, because I have a feeling finishing the house tour will take up the remainder of my day.

I pause, allowing Ms. Amelia a moment before I get out of my car. I also take my time walking to the passenger's side to retrieve my bag. I don't want Ms. Amelia thinking I'm watching her, and I certainly don't want to make her more uncomfortable than she already is. She's already extremely terrified. Joining her at the stairs, I smile. She turns and looks at me with tired eyes.

"Let's get this over with," she says, swinging the front door open.

Chapter 10

*"The Lord is close to the brokenhearted; He rescues
those whose spirits are crushed."*

– Psalm 34:18

As Ms. Amelia and I ascend the grand staircase, I get a feeling of déjà vu. We reach the landing and turn in unison to gaze at the lovely stained-glass window. I'm in admiration of its art, beauty, and grandeur. She pauses, catching her breath, as if doing so will give her more strength for what's to come. Straightening her shoulders, she points matter-of-factly saying, "Megan, we will begin here in my chapel at the end of the hall. Then, as we make our way back downstairs, we'll stop in each of the bedrooms."

As we walk down the spacious hallway, I take in as much as I can; three double doors line each side of the grand hallway, along with more lovely paintings adorning the walls, cleverly mixed with pictures of her children for a grand total of thirteen. The walls here look just like the walls in the foyer, giving cohesiveness from the stairs to the hallway. Thankful that my phone is on silent, I take a few pictures of the architectural details, being careful to keep as many antiques out of the pictures as possible. I slowly and in a very casual and relaxed way sweep my phone from one side to another, while also being careful to keep Ms. Amelia out of the photos.

We reach the beautiful double doors at the end of the hallway, which are flanked by tall three-paned windows. The only difference between these thick, mahogany doors and all the others is the beautifully carved crosses in the middle of them.

The chapel is literally a round tower attached to the side of the house. Ms. Amelia reverently opens the doors wide, and we step into another world! My mouth drops open in awe! It is exactly as I imagined it would be.

A cozy, old-world, stone chapel with white marble floors and mahogany pews are before me. There is a vaulted cathedral ceiling and a plush, rich red carpet runner spanning the entire middle aisle straight to the altar at the front. On each side of the aisle are seven red-cushioned pews. Lining the chapel walls are gorgeous detailed paintings depicting the birth, life, ministry, death, and resurrection of Jesus Christ. At the front of the chapel, spanning from ceiling to floor above the altar is the most glorious chiseled marble statue of Jesus' ascension into heaven that I have ever seen!

"Do you like my chapel, Megan?"

As I stand in complete reverence and amazement, a single, "Wow!" is all I can manage. The chapel's design is so perfect, and its condition so pristine, you'd never know you were in a house. I am still taking it all in as Ms. Amelia leads me to a cushioned pew, and we sit. Sunlight pouring into the chapel adds a warm glow to the room. I sit in silent appreciation, not daring to make a sound.

I'm finally able to find a few words, but they don't seem to be enough. "Ms. Amelia, this is breathtaking! I absolutely love it!" For a moment I forget the real reason I am here.

"Thank you. Yes, it is. This is truly my sanctuary," she says, almost whispering.

Ms. Amelia is quite calm, and a relaxed yet radiant smile comes to her face as she begins speaking with loving fondness of her chapel. She begins by pointing out everything, telling me where each piece has come from, and seems quite excited to tell me about the items that were given to her for free!

"Free?!?" I ask in disbelief. I am shocked! "Why, however

did you get these magnificent items for free?"

This prompts a delightful story about the time Daisy, Ms. Amelia, and the sisters traveled to a small town three hours away. The town's art gallery had a painting Ms. Amelia was to pick up for a client. Daisy had been researching chapels and their varying designs depending on the time period they were constructed, the cultural atmosphere, and the country in which they were built. Through a contact, she had been notified of a parish in the same town who was selling some items in their chapel.

"Daisy and the sisters tagged along with me, because they thought the town showed the promise of a few stores that possibly had pieces they were looking for, plus we all wanted to sneak a peek at the items at the parish sale. So, they all went with me. On the way, we spotted an auction sign in front of a sad and weathered-down church. After confirming this was the same parish Daisy had wanted to look at, we stopped. The priest was there, and he told us the story of how attendance was down, and that the upkeep was getting to be too much. A newer parish nearby was expanding, however, and it was decided that he and the other priest would soon be sharing duties of the joined congregations. The priest started crying, thinking of seeing these pieces that had been blessed by God auctioned off. I still laugh when I remember Sister Margaretta interrupting the priest with childlike excitement telling him what we were doing at my home. By the end of her story, the priest let us take whatever we wanted, after he blessed us all. I, of course, wrote a generous check and told him to use it as he needed and to share with anyone else who may have a financial need."

As we move around the chapel, Ms. Amelia lovingly keeps repeating how the sisters of the parish made it their mission to give her this place of rest and relaxation. I was pleased to see her so calm, joyful, and peaceful, a stark contrast from when she'd burst into the office building this morning and the first time I'd come across her.

"Megan, they took it upon themselves to be my guardian angels of sorts. First, it was simply the planning and designing of the chapel, then it was little outings with Daisy and my kids to find our chapel treasures, and after the dedication service, the sisters found a way to come for weekly prayer luncheons. I needed those days. Luther had gradually turned into an angry man, or maybe he'd always been that way but had hidden it from me. Or, I'd missed the signs. Anyway, he'd leave every day early in the morning and arrive in the middle of dinner exceptionally drunk. We didn't talk much anymore, and since life didn't seem to be going his way, he would drunkenly take it all out on me, screaming, yelling, and yes, sometimes hinting or slapping me if I challenged or questioned him. Somehow, at some point in a drunken rant, it would end up being all my fault, even if it wasn't about me."

She winces at the memories going through her mind. "I finally learned what I needed to do in order to survive, and found refuge in peace and calm. I was surviving, but I was not living. And yes, Megan, they are two very different things. Back then, if you sought counseling, people saw you as a failure. If you confided in church leaders, it was *you* who'd sinned, not the person who chose to abuse you. So, naturally, you can understand, Megan, why I was at a loss for what to do. Thankfully, many in our world today no longer turn a blind eye to spousal abuse, and support is much easier to come by. These strong, brave souls are exposing the truth, being a beacon of light and supporting people who need to escape from their abusers. I'm sure there were people back then who would have helped me and even counseled me, but I learned to trust no one until recently."

She pauses, gathering her thoughts. "Anyway, years later, once things got really bad and it was apparent the supportive town folks had turned their back on me and I could not leave the house, the sisters and the priest would hold a service here in the chapel for me and the kids, if they were in town visiting. Then we would share a meal together afterward. It seems they simply couldn't get away from our chapel, and I didn't want them to stay away, either."

She gets up and moves in the direction of the altar, and I am compelled to follow.

"Megan, if you kneel here and look closely at the altar, you'll see the verse from Psalms, chapter 34, verse 18 is carved into it. This was Daisy's idea, and John did the carving! It took me a long time to take those words to heart, to believe them, and let Him, the God of our universe, love me and rescue me in a way."

"The Lord is close to the brokenhearted; He rescues
those whose spirits are crushed."

I nod as the words I just read sink in, and settle in for some more wisdom.

"I've learned, when we take pause and stop all the noise in our life, when we really evaluate everything in our life closely and ponder which decision feels best, we start to see how we are led in the right direction and can make decisions that are best for us. However, many times we're too busy to ponder a choice, letting desire before common sense take over, and we instead jump in with both feet too quickly. If more people would learn to slow down, their lives wouldn't be in such chaos. We are allowed to choose for ourselves what path we take, but God does know an easier route if we'd swallow our pride and learn to listen. Our priest once shared a parable with me."

I notice Ms. Amelia shifting nervously, as she continues.

"A man's house was flooding. He prayed, and cried out for help. Soon, a neighbor came by in his motor boat wanting the man to join him, but he declined, saying God would help him. This happened two more times, and after the third time, the waters swept him under. Arriving at the pearly gates, he was very angry, and asked the angel why God didn't rescue him. The angel answered, 'God was there and did try to help you; don't you remember? He sent your neighbor, then the coast guard, and finally a search and rescue helicopter, but you chose not to accept their help.' That was powerful for me, Megan. This is why I still hold onto a little hope and can never be mad at God. Oh, I was at first. I was angry and asked God why He did this to me. With the help and prayers of the Sisters, I learned God didn't do this to me, I chose to marry whom I did. Please know, I am *not* making excuses for what he did. Through it all, God was still with me helping me through, or I wouldn't be alive and in the mentally stable state I am in today. People want to say it's by their own hard work, sweat, and tears that they got to where they are, that they didn't need God. Well, who kept giving you the air you breathe? Who gave you the desire or faith to keep moving forward? Many times, it takes a disaster or a loss of something or someone before we start slowing down and listening to our heart or our gut instincts."

I follow Ms. Amelia's eyes as they travel the pictures of Christ's journey to the cross. "Megan, many will argue with me, some shake their head in disbelief, but this is my own journey. This obviously doesn't sell my home, but it does help me heal, and lets you know why I am somehow at peace with it all. And, being innocent helps too," she adds with a wink, smiling.

She gets up and I am compelled to follow. She walks behind the altar to a beautiful marble statue of Mother Mary sitting. At Mary's feet, there is a plush, velvet, rose-colored pillow. Pointing, Ms. Amelia quietly says, "I was right here when I got the news that Luther had died. I was also here when I got the news that I would be going back in for more questioning by the police, as if it was still my fault. I was here praying, when I was told by John that it was, in fact, Anita's daughter who was found dead in our car at the bottom of the river. Anita was the only widow who was ungrateful, who had made it her mission to get even with Luther and me after the death of her husband. Even after Luther and I had paid all three widows generous money that would've been theirs anyway had their husbands lived to complete their contracts, Anita was the only one who never seemed to let it go and to blame us for the unfortunate accident. Even after she remarried, she seemed to sneak around events we'd attend, and tried to get caught with Luther."

I can tell she needs to tell me this, so I just listen, knowing it will make her feel better and just might get me closer to the truth of the Beauregard mystery.

"Now, Luther was very controlling of me and violent when intoxicated. He knew who he was married to, and the family that stood behind me." Her eyes cloud over as she pauses, comforting herself before she mutters painfully, "I guess not even I nor my father's wealth and upstanding name could keep him from financial temptation. That is a person's choice and it comes from deep within the human soul, Megan."

She sighs deeply, sitting down in a pew, and continues telling me how Anita always seemed to be around. The night it happened, Ms. Amelia was "volunteering" at the store while Luther went to the town board meeting to discuss a housing development and a new addition to the school. The housing development would impact one of the main roads. Luther had also mentioned they would be talking about the usual logistics, funding, layout, and name for the new road. While she was working, a wife of one of the board members had come into the store looking distraught and very confused. Ms. Amelia laughs and shakes her head before her eyes cloud over.

"Megan, she was confused because she couldn't figure out how I'd gotten to the store so quickly. I told her how long I had been there, and the woman proceeded to tell me how she'd dropped her husband off at the town hall and saw me talking with Luther. I insisted I'd been at work the whole time. The woman shook her head and continued her shopping, but I continued puzzling over how she could think she saw me speaking with my husband while I had been at work. Then, a short time later, Anita's daughter and some of her friends came into the store to pick up her mother's order. They were excitedly talking about the high school football game they'd be attending, and when she saw me, she exclaimed that her mother was wearing the same outfit as me! After a few more hours passed, I helped close the store at 5 pm. I went straight home, showered, changed clothes, and then headed to my chapel to pray."

Amelia pauses, as if lost within a troubling thought, to watch the sunlight dance over the ornate nativity scene she said her kids had picked out. *I wonder if she is thinking, praying, or searching for words?*

Finally, Ms. Amelia finds her hidden strength and begins again. "Sister Margaret had come with the other two sisters from the parish to check on me, and it was here on this cushion where they found me. During the time, I had thought it odd and was rather startled that John had let them come up, but even more so that they'd ventured out at night, and especially during the convent's sacred evening prayers. But, Megan, they were so dead set on being with me. And then all hell broke loose, and I was so incredibly grateful they were right there…here… with me."

Then, as if more horrible memories are too much to handle, Ms. Amelia stands and walks over to sit in another pew, and I get the feeling she is done talking for a while. I reverently make my way around the room admiring the paintings. When Amelia isn't looking, I take a few more pictures, again being careful to keep her out of them. I soon begin seeing the same pattern that is constant throughout the entire house, the groupings of three or the evidence of seven. Three chandeliers, each resembling a king's crown, hang above the seven pews on the left side and the same on the right, with the final chandelier hanging down over the altar at the front. It hangs high enough that from the doors coming in, it looks as if Jesus is wearing a gold crown! There are three clouds with Jesus as He ascends into heaven.

The paintings around the chapel are grouped in threes, and there are seven candles on the ornate table to the far left of the altar. I remember the double doors coming into the chapel have a cross on each door, but that would make only two. I turn around, chuckling as I look. When the doors are shut, there is, in fact, a smaller third cross in the middle, for a total of three. I smile as I think about how much thought, time, and love has been put into this entire estate, Ms. Amelia's refuge of peace. *I can't forget to ask Ms. Amelia about the importance of the numbers three and seven, since she has not offered it up again.* I have a strong feeling I must be specific with these particular questions.

Ms. Amelia has been quiet during my self-guided tour around the chapel, so I move to the pew in front of her, where I can look at her, and we both can sit comfortably and chat. "Ms. Amelia, please explain your fondness for the numbers three and seven. I'm still quite curious, and you did promise you'd tell me."

"It really has nothing to do with the sale of my home, but since I promised, I will explain."

"Do you not think someone touring the home is bound to take notice, Ms. Amelia?"

"Well, Megan, up until that fateful night, many people had come and gone from my home, but only a few family members have ever inquired about the meaning of my numbers. So, if anyone does ask, we will take it as a sign!" *Hmm, that's an interesting way to go about this.*

"Okay, Megan, here is the answer to your question. Three and seven are my numbers. I never want to hear them referred to as my *lucky* numbers, ever. They are simply my numbers. Why? Well, everything good in my life has happened in threes and sevens, or they have happened right at three or seven o'clock, even 3:03 and 7:07. In a time in my life when I needed to feel in control of what was happening around me, I chose to focus on and honor those two numbers in my life and all throughout my home. The ancient Greek philosopher, Pythagoras, insisted that the meaning behind numbers was deeply significant. In his eyes the number three was considered the perfect number. It was seen as the number of harmony, wisdom, understanding, strength, and beauty.

Within Christendom, there is significant meaning and symbolism in numbers as well. We speak of the Holy Trinity, for example. Or speak of the angelic number three being closely linked to feelings of hope and optimism. Many believe their futures look bright if they see this number. If you study numerology, which I find quite fascinating, and there too, the number three is a representation of wisdom and balance, and regarded as a sign of originality and openness to the world."

Ms. Amelia eyes me with curiosity, trying to read my face, so I nod in utter fascination. Satisfied, she continues.

"So, because my 'thing for numbers' was seen as kind of weird, and no one had the desire to question me, I was often allowed to humor myself and tweak the architect's designs to fit my liking. Partially because it entertained me how much it amused him, and partially because anything ornate and fun granted him more business. If you think back to each story, where I've mentioned the numbers three and seven, they have all been happy and or ended well. Even the years these events all took place ended in three or seven!"

Suddenly, the three builders come to mind, and I hear myself questioning Ms. Amelia's own statement. "Please forgive me, Ms. Amelia, I don't mean to be rude. What about the three builders who died?"

She grins. "Those three didn't die at the same time. The years and months in which they died, even the days and times..." she shudders. "They were not in threes or sevens. I paired the men together, so they could be honored for their craftsmanship, skills, and hard work. While alive, they made an excellent team when working together, and as soon as I realized this, I grouped them together on as many projects around the house as I could. Things were going very well... until Luther took it upon himself to split them up, having them each work on separate projects.

And this, my dear, is when the troubles began. After their deaths and the house was completely finished, I honored their memory at the same time, by grouping them back together. Thus, honoring their devotion to their families and the building of our house. This, in my heart, righted their unfortunate events in a way. Or, at least I like to think so."

She looks at me, trying to find words. "Megan, I don't expect you to understand it all, because it does feel weird to me to explain the thoughts that keep me grounded and sane. Yet, at the same time, I trust that in many ways you do understand, or you wouldn't be inquiring. Even recently on the stairs, I sensed you counting along with me, and you noticed that our evening didn't end well and that our numbers were not three and seven either. Well, there you have it! Call me superstitious, but paying attention to these extra details have kept me alert and grounded."

Opening her purse, Ms. Amelia pulls out two wrapped Danish pastries from the local coffee shop, handing one to me. "Megan, let's have a bite to eat before we continue our tour, shall we?" Bowing her head, she prays a humble blessing over our lunch and the remainder of our afternoon.

Lord, hear our prayer.

Chapter 11

"Yesterday is gone. Tomorrow has not yet come.
We only have today. Let us begin."

– Mother Teresa

Ms. Amelia pauses as we exit the chapel, as if trying to decide in which bedroom to begin. As she slowly veers to the left side of the hallway, she lets me know the bedrooms are all the same size, with two of them connected by a decent-sized bathroom. On the opposite side of the hallway sits the master bedroom with a lovely en-suite, walk-in closet, and sitting room. This is followed further along the hall by the guest bedroom closest to the chapel, which also has its own bathroom.

In the first bedroom, Ms. Amelia smiles as she reminisces about her sweet child who once occupied this room. One glance at Ms. Amelia with her look of joy and happiness and I am grateful John has kept the rooms very well maintained and tidy for her. The furniture chosen for each room is a perfect blend of new and old classical pieces that have stood the test of time. Ms. Amelia lets me know that her children picked out their furniture and pictures plus, whatever else has been added to the room over the years is now theirs to keep. Over time, the rooms have transitioned well, so that when the kids come home to visit, they and their families stay in these rooms. I make a few notes while I am listening, writing down the measurements, as well as looking for new dust prints, vacuum marks, foot indentions in the carpet, finger prints, or anything out of the ordinary that stands out to me.

I feel my inner detective could surface at any time. These rooms have stories untold.

After a few more stories and some laughs in the other bedroom, she looks at me with hesitation, and I swear I see tears well up in her eyes. Silently, she moves across the hall, and time seems to stand still. As she finally opens the door, I can instantly see why. This is the master bedroom she and Luther once shared. Again, I can see that good, reliable John has done a prodigious job with the up-keep in here...*No dust, it's vacuumed... I really don't have to worry about staging very much in Ms. Amelia's home. Every room is already absolutely perfect!*

Moments later, we're still standing in the doorway. Ms. Amelia is finding the courage to go inside. "Megan, this is the first time I've stepped into this room since... the week after Luther's funeral." Then she gasps, realizing how clean the room is. "Oh, hasn't John done a lovely job of keeping everything looking so fresh and elegant after all these years? Everything is right where I left it!"

Her reaction settles some hesitations I've had about how trustworthy I think John really is, but it still leaves me confused. Just as I'd done in each of the other rooms, I look around one last time. I leave nothing unseen, because I am also acting as Sherlock would, and I still need a few more clues for London.

Ms. Amelia helps me finish taking measurements, as well as recites many others from memory. As we sit in the alcove by the beautiful bay window, we discuss some ideas on how we can keep all of her treasures from being stolen. I'd already taken pictures of every room, closet, hallways, stairways...everything. While Ms. Amelia thinks our ideas over, I pray for some creative answers and that if I should think of any, they will be accepted by Ms. Amelia.

Then, I see it! One bedside table has a drawer that is not fully shut! A chill runs down my spine...something is out of place!

I know we're about done with the house tour, and I have a feeling I'd better think of something quick to start talking about, or down the stairs we'll go, and out I'll go. An idea comes. "Ms. Amelia, how do you feel about packing up the art pieces you've willed your children along with some of the other treasures and furniture pieces throughout your home that are extremely valuable? If we need to, we would then replace your items with items we borrow from our staging team?" She nods, so I continue. "Would it be possible to have your children come pick up their items before I officially list the house? This way none of their precious belongings are lost in shipping, stolen, or broken, and you can move forward with the sale of your estate. Your children will personally be given their items, and you will have peace of mind knowing all your valuables are safe within your children's care."

"What a wonderful idea, Megan!"

What a relief! I'm so glad I'm off to a great start! As she excitedly bounces off a few suggestions for implementing this plan, I put it in our company calendar so we can begin working out a date for scheduling a showing.

"Ms. Amelia, would we be able to do the same in the rest of the house? I'm sure this will put your mind at ease."

"Yes, if you'll be able to help me. Since John is in jail, I need all the help I can get."

This is brilliant! I will, of course, because this scores me a couple more days on the estate! Oooh, Sherlock this has to be considered a break in the case, but only time will tell!

"It will be an honor to help you with this project, Ms. Amelia. When would you like us to begin?" Still sitting in the alcove, I let Ms. Amelia watch as I email the pictures and measurements of each room to Mona and our company's stager. This way they can come in after we pack things up and make quick work of the job. It will also mean less anxiety for Ms. Amelia, giving her the peace of mind that her treasures are safe with her children, and gives Mona a chance to come to the estate.

She looks quite relieved and pleased. "Megan, shall we start tomorrow morning?"

As I glance at a work email, I notice Ms. Amelia again wiping tears from her eyes. This room, no doubt, is filled with a ton of emotions. With respect, I verbally and lovingly applaud her bravery. I remind her of tomorrow, hoping it will bring the promise of happiness and peace that is coming her way.

"Megan, I've been working through some long-suppressed emotions just now. It makes me sad to pack up my memories, even though I know I should. But yesterday is gone, and I hold all the memories in my heart, both the good and the bad. Today is what I've been blessed with, along with the chance of tomorrow, which brings hope. And that, dearie, gives me peace."

Suddenly, a change comes over Ms. Amelia. Her eyes turn stony and cold, and despite her term of endearment for me, I intuitively sense that she doesn't trust me for some reason. A feeling of panic wells up inside me.

"Megan," she begins suddenly with a stern undertone, "Why do you sound so confident that happiness and peace are coming my way? Do you know something I don't know? You know you must tell me now, or I am finished! I will not be fraternized or coddled in my own home!"

I begin praying that I am maintaining a calm cool expression on my face, while at the same time considering what my reply should be. I decide it's best to give the same reassuring reply I did back at the office. It feels better that way, to be consistent and stand in the integrity of what I've already said. *For some people, change is a difficult thing to master. And if, in fact, Ms. Amelia is one of those people, less will be more.*

Maybe I can redirect Ms. Amelia while cheering her up, by reminding her there are two final areas on the estate to be seen? "Ms. Amelia, why don't we walk to the remaining areas of the estate.

I'm eager to see the patio with its garden off the kitchen and the grove of trees I spotted from the driveway."

"Let's go then!" her smile returns, and I take the opportunity to ask Ms. Amelia about the slightly open drawer.

"Do you remember what you used to keep in there?" I intended to be casual, as if I'd just glanced over and noticed it open.

I clearly startled her, because she turns around with panic in her eyes, collapsing into the nearest chair.

"Oh, I pray to God, there was nothing of importance left here by either Luther or me!" She gets up and moves to the dresser.

London's voice bellows into my subconscious. "Stop!" I command rather alarmingly, to both of us. "I'm so sorry, Ms. Amelia, but in light of all the recent happenings, we shouldn't touch anything. If somehow someone did get in and snooped around, we might just have their fingerprints!"

She mulls this over for a bit before conceding, "Well, Megan, what are you waiting for? Zoom in with your camera and take some pictures of the floor near the bedside table, and of the bedside table itself. Then we'll go to the patio!"

With amusement, I quickly do as I'm told, handing her my phone so she can see each photo once I'm done. After she gives her approval of the pictures, we make our way downstairs.

Ms. Amelia slows down as we walk onto the patio. She pauses a moment and snaps off a few flowers to take along with us. "Megan, we're going to start in the grove of trees first, while no one is here but us."

There is a respectful way to how she walks. I can almost feel the heavy sadness within each step she takes on the way to the grove of trees. It takes us only a couple of minutes to reach the grove, and we walk up to the small, elegantly manicured cemetery. I bow my head in respect, suddenly getting the feeling I'm intruding on something. Glancing out of the corner of my eye, I watch as Ms. Amelia lovingly pays her respects, quietly says some prayers, and places a flower on each headstone. Each marble headstone is very clean and in pristine condition. N*o doubt this is John's handiwork.* While she lingers at each, I look around to make sure we are, in fact, by ourselves.

"Megan, I feel like, with the sales of the estate, I am actually turning my back on the sisters and Daisy in a way. It's like they instinctively knew Luther was getting violent. I knew something was off, but thought his mayoral position in town was causing him great amounts of stress. It was, but I later learned that on top of that my first husband had been pestering him, asking about some papers, and if he knew about them or their location. If you aren't strong enough, you can eventually give in to evil and let it take over you. And that's just what happened with Luther."

I listen with eagerness, knowing that I am getting closer to the answers I want.

"I later learned that Luther and my ex had plotted this huge scheme against me which led to the whole catastrophe. I am so thankful my kids were married and had their own lives by that time. As much as Anita meddled around in our lives, I wouldn't be surprised if she was in on the scheme as well. She was the head librarian then and seemed to keep a sharp eye on us. At town events, if I wasn't arm-in-arm with Luther she'd find a way to get beside him, even though they were both married."

I interrupt. "Ms. Amelia, can you describe Anita, and do you know if she's retired from her position at the library?"

To my shock, Ms. Amelia describes the woman at the library who had raised the hairs on my neck. *That woman is Anita!* To maintain transparency with Ms. Amelia, I share my library experience I had with Anita. As I do, I feel as if letting her know what had happened in the library has just brought us a little closer. *I still cannot fathom how an entire town could go against one woman for all these years, after listening to these stories.*

Amelia must have read my mind. "I might as well tell you everything I know about the night that led to my fate. Do you remember when I said a customer asked how I'd gotten to work so quickly, since she'd seen me over at the town hall a mere few minutes earlier?"

I nod, and she continues.

"I may have said this before, and even one of the nuns mentioned later, Anita and I had been wearing the exact same outfit that day! Back then, we were about the same size and shape, and with it being dark, there was one hundred percent chance we could've been mistaken for each other, especially from a distance. I had chosen not to attend the town hall event that night because I was helping the store owner seal a deal with a big customer. I waited until the afternoon to phone Luther at his office. I lied and told him I wasn't feeling my best and would be staying home that night. Up until then, he didn't know I had a job, and thought I only volunteered one day a week at the store. Well, since I was no longer going to the event at the town hall that night, it was the perfect time for them to initiate the plan they'd been working on for ages. It became apparent that their plan was to frame me for stealing, blame John as my accomplice, and get us both locked up in jail. Anita's allegiance was really to Hunter. Seems she played a lot of men - she was only interested in a relationship with Luther so she could get into the house and get what Hunter needed. She connived, constructed, and agreed to give him access to the house so he could take what he wanted..."

She adopts a mischievous grin, "However, that wasn't entirely what happened. Anita had been very successful with making it appear to the entire town that she and I hated each other. Yet, truth be told, I never hated her. I simply avoided her because I knew she blamed me for everything that had happened when her first husband died, and I would never be able to make her see any differently."

She stops, taking a deep breath. "On that fateful night, Luther took our going-out car instead of his own. This meant, and was known through the entire town, that either one of us could have driven it. After Anita was seen looking like me by a few people, she must have slipped into our car to wait for Luther. Now, John and I have replayed countless scenarios over the years, and this one I'm giving you is as close to what we think happened, taking into careful consideration what Gabe was able to share with us once he retired."

She takes another deep breath, clasping her hands together, as if preparing herself for what's to come. "Okay, so she must have waited in the car for an hour or so before Luther joined her in the car, and he and Anita hurriedly drove toward her house so she could change. They mustn't have used any headlights, because they didn't want anyone to see or recognize the car. Sadly, because of that, they weren't able to see the young woman on the side of the road in the dark, and tragically they ran over her. Even worse, she was Anita's daughter!"

By now I'm crying, and so is Ms. Amelia. We are cuddled up near the sisters' headstones, as if by doing so we will find comfort. If anyone is currently snooping around now I wouldn't know it, because I am thoroughly absorbed in Ms. Amelia's story. Sherlock senses be damned!

Ms. Amelia sobs, then regains control. "Megan, that Friday night was absolutely awful! Anita's daughter had been to the football game at the school, and decided at the last minute to walk home instead of staying the weekend at her friend's house. We think she had maybe dropped something and was bent down intently searching for it. That's the only way to explain how they hit her. So, not knowing what they'd hit, and also not wanting to be seen together, Luther and Anita continued driving."

At this, her motherly instinct kicks in and she starts crying at the awful thought, and I am still crying.

"Her sweet daughter, God rest her soul, managed to stumble off to the side of the road into high grasses, before God in His mercy, spared her from any more suffering. Forensics determined she likely died along the side of the road. Thinking they'd hit an animal or run over a log, Luther and Anita continued on until the car started acting up. As fate would have it, the steering gave out, running them into a deep, murky ditch."

I gasp in amazement "It's astonishing they didn't realize it was much more than a log! How could they not know?!"

"One would think it would be apparent given the fact they ran over something pretty large, but they must've been very distracted and hurried. With their precious plans now messed up, and the car filling with water, they climbed out and walked. Anita went to her house and Luther to ours. I now laugh thinking of how much walking they did that night in the dark! Luther changed out of his muddy clothes. Not wanting me to find them, he wrapped them in a trash bag and hid it in his closet, before getting into his own car, and rushing back over to pick up Anita so they could finish carrying out their evil plan. We suppose Anita changed out of her wet and muddy clothes too, putting them in the dryer, before changing into a house dress and staying home long enough for the neighbor to realize she was at home. She made some calls from her house phone, went to the mailbox, even took a cake over to an elderly neighbor. From what we could piece together, she changed back into the dress that looked like mine and waited for Luther."

"Holy moly, Ms. Amelia! If this doesn't scream premeditated, I don't know what does!" I was trying to wrap my head around it all. Ms. Amelia had had years to make sense of these events, and it was a lot for me to take in.

"Yes, it does seem premeditated because most of it was! So, during all of this, Anita's darling husband was still at the event at the town hall, oblivious to everything his wife was doing. Luther stopped back by the event so it would appear he'd been there the whole time, and then he slipped out again.

I still get chills thinking that, for God knows how long, my ex-husband, or someone, had to have been watching me, following me, listening, taking notes before this night. And even that day someone was following me, so they could tell Anita which dress I was wearing, yet we still aren't certain how they managed to do it! I've often wondered how many dresses like mine she owned.

"If that seems crazy... well, buckle up, there's even more! After all this, Luther and Anita went over to the local art gallery to steal a painting Luther knew I loved. Now, this part of their zany plan worked. The security alarm was tripped, sirens rang out, and Anita ran. The security cameras showed the back of the dress, and she was careful not to show her face to them as she ran. She also managed to get away. Meanwhile, after dropping Anita off in the back alley near the gallery, Luther had gone back over to the town hall to officially adjourn the meeting."

"This makes my head spin, Ms. Amelia. Where were you the whole time that was going on?"

"Unfortunately, the break-in occurred during the precise time I took my dinner break at work. Whenever I took my breaks, I would always sit in my car and listen to music on the radio while I ate my lunch, relaxed, and regrouped. I'd look through the paper, or write a letter to my kids or my parents. I always took my meal breaks alone. I tell you, someone had to have known my every move, because Luther didn't even know I worked there...yet! And, Megan, I'm sure you can figure out the rest of the story."

I open my mouth to speak, but she isn't finished and continues on. I have no idea about the rest of the story, to be honest, so I might as well keep quiet and listen.

"I eventually had to confess to having the job to Luther. He was irate and began telling anyone who would listen that I was not to be trusted and was a chronic liar. The police and prosecutors, of course, questioned specific witnesses who testified under oath that they'd seen me both places, and yet, there was no forensic evidence to tie me to either of the crime scenes! To my relief, the police eventually let me go after quite lengthy questioning, but only after getting another warrant, and searching my entire house again. I assumed that since it was, without a doubt, proven the painting wasn't at our home, and none of their arguments could even be proven, I'd be "forgiven" by my town. Sadly, no. We think Anita must have given the stolen painting to my ex, who then turned around and sold it for a hefty sum of money, because to this day, no one has located it!"

A chill runs down my spine, and I suddenly become cold. Ms. Amelia gets up, heading for the sunny spot on the patio. She continues her story as we walk.

"Their plan ended up being even better than they'd imagined. There were so many questions left unanswered that the detective spent days trying to tie all the events together into one heck of a story. Here we had Anita's daughter missing, our going-out car missing, the idea that John was at home and could conveniently hide evidence, combined with no one seeing me for an hour while I was on my break at work, and a painting no one could ever find, which left the only question no one ever asked, why and how could I have taken two cars while doing everything that night, especially in the allotted time they said it all happened?"

"And, with all of this you still ended up being their only suspect, Ms. Amelia? They didn't even consider any other possibilities? How ridiculous!"

"Yes, indeed it was. Poor John was subjected to intense interrogation unmercifully. Finally, they gave him a lie detector test, and it proved he was telling the truth, but the town was still not convinced about me! John was quickly released and cleared from any wrongdoing and welcomed back into the town's good graces. Well, mostly. As it turned out, when my father and his attorney helped me update my will, it was cleverly reworded, so that if John was caught disobeying the law, anything that had been willed to him would be canceled. I guess this proved to the jury that John wouldn't have done anything untoward. At this point, he was let go and his name was cleared. And I was begrudgingly let go because there wasn't physical proof that I'd stolen the painting or killed Anita's daughter."

"It amazes me, no one ever truly dug into this more than they did."

"Megan, you'd be surprised at how many cases were handled like this back then. And, please remember, no matter what people may tell you, all I've shared regarding what happened has been the result of countless years of revisiting it in my mind or replaying it over sandwiches and seemingly endless pitchers of sweet tea here on the patio with John, Gabe, and his sweet wife. The problem we still have, is finding someone to reopen the case, someone who believes that it does indeed need to happen. Gabe actually tried reopening the case a few years later, but his theory seemed such a stretch to the powers that be, and without enough 'fresh eyes' on the case and no theory of their own, not a single person believed him. It wasn't long after that that people began treating him and his wife badly for standing up for me. I tell you Megan, I am innocent, but not in the town's eyes."

"Ms. Amelia, this injustice and lack of respect for the law is absolutely shocking. Do you know how much London knows, or if his opinion has been tainted in any way?"

"Smart question, Megan, but I'm sorry to say I don't actually know." She gets a little quieter and leans closer. "Around a year after things died down, Luther went on one of his weekend business trips, and I stayed home. John and I did the usual annual spring clean, and it was then that we found Luther's bag of clothes he'd hidden in the back of his closet. They were so stinky and moldy, but John was confident this evidence would at least prove Luther was part of something that had happened that night. He hoped this fresh evidence would be enough to clear me. Wasting no time, he ran straight to the police station expecting to clear my name and show that it was Luther and not me who had some connection to that fateful Friday evening involving Anita's daughter's death. I thought we'd gotten lucky."

For a moment, she looks at me with the sadness of decades before saying more.

"Forensics tests showed that it was possible the dirt on his clothes came from that ditch. Soon, investigators began canvassing the area and found our going-out car, along with Anita's daughter inside! The new clues now gave the police and the town a fresh perspective, but the question now was, how did Anita's daughter get inside the car? John, Gabe and I thought I'd surely be exonerated at least from her death, since there was still nothing to show I had been in the car that night. Since it was already clear John couldn't have been my accomplice, it seemed even more likely that it would be clear it couldn't have been me involved. What also became clear is that the car could have been driven an entirely different route to what had been supposed. This in turn debunked the probability that I would have been capable of getting from work and back within my break time without anyone noticing I was gone."

"Wow, Ms. Amelia, it sounds like it could have been solved with a little more sleuthing, right then and there!"

"Even still, with all the literal proof falling into place, no one was convinced. To make my nightmare worse, they formed a new theory involving Luther, placing him as my driver and accomplice! No one considered it could possibly be someone other than me. They started a new hypothesis, saying I was so mad at Anita that I wanted revenge, and her daughter had unfortunately gotten in the way as I escaped with the painting! It was awful! My lawyer thought this theory was preposterous, and assumed with the new judge presiding over the court it would be an open and shut case. He was sure the evidence was sufficient for me to be cleared. But it was still not so. Thankfully, though, a few parts of the DA's theory were debunked, and their third search at our house found something more that tied it all to Luther, because he was then asked to report home for questioning."

I couldn't contain my excitement. This was like watching a suspenseful drama unfold, right on the sunny patio. "Good heavens, what did they find? What was it?"

"Two days later, when Luther hadn't returned from his business trip, they contacted me to see if he'd been in touch with me. They still thought I was involved and that he was my accomplice so they thought I might be harboring him somewhere. When they called, I of course gave the police the address of the hotel and the room number he was supposedly staying in. Truthfully, I didn't think he'd actually be there. But, when the police went to arrest him, they confirmed what I had felt but didn't want to believe. It was worse than thinking he'd escaped with Anita...he had committed suicide!"

I gasp, and poor Ms. Amelia jumps.

"Obviously, recent fingerprints of mine were not found on either car, but they most certainly found Luther's fingerprints all over his car and the going-out car. Not to mention incriminating man-sized handprint marks on Anita's daughter's body, God rest her soul. This gave the police proof he'd driven the car and had placed Anita's daughter's body inside the trunk of the car to hide her. We pieced together the timeline and determined that it was likely that Luther had gone back to the scene to see what he had hit. When he searched and found Anita's daughter's body off in the tall grass, he must have dragged her into the trunk of the car to hide the body."

"Oh my gosh! This is horrible! But, Ms. Amelia, I have a question if I may. Why, after all of the evidence that *still* doesn't point to you, do the authorities still believe you were somehow involved in this ghastly crime?"

She opens her mouth to answer me, only to be stopped by beautiful melodious chimes, letting her know someone is at the front gate. She scurries into the kitchen and heads to the security panel on the wall. Placing her hand over her heart and pressing the button, she speaks a cautious greeting.

To my utter shock, I hear London's stern voice blare through the speaker. "Ms. Amelia, it's London from the police department! I ask that you let me in immediately."

Ms. Amelia goes white. "Uh, yes sir," she hesitates as she presses the button.

I had never seen Ms. Amelia so suddenly out of control and visibly shaken before. She quickly turns to me, handing me a single key. "Megan," she whispers. "Take my extra house key. It's four o'clock, and I have a bad feeling about this. Nothing good happens at four o'clock for me, and I have a feeling someone has tried to pin something on me again, knowing that selling the estate means I am likely to be leaving town. What they don't realize is that I now have you. I pray you have a sharp mind and can keep your wits about you, because if something goes wrong, I need you to continue with our estate plans regardless."

I stare down at the key in my hand.

"This key will let you in this back patio door. Upon being inserted into the keyhole, it will disarm the security alarm, signaling all is well. Once you're inside and lock the patio door again, the alarm system will focus on the windows, doors, and the perimeter of the house. Oh, I need you to…" She stops when a heavy knock sounds on the front door.

I follow her, still in utter shock and disbelief. I am speechless and at a loss for words.

"Open up, Ms. Amelia," comes London's deep voice. As soon as she opens the door, we hear him say, "You are once again under arrest for the murder of…"

Chapter 12

"It's a capital mistake to theorize before one has data. Insensibly, one begins to twist facts to suit theories, instead of theories to suit facts..."

– Sherlock Holmes, A Scandal in Bohemia

In an instant, everything fades away and my mind and soul are flooded with emotions. I feel this is incredibly wrong, and feel utterly helpless knowing there is nothing I can do to help. Even though I've known her only a short time, deep within my soul, I know Ms. Amelia is telling me the truth and didn't have anything to do with the death of Anita's daughter. Gabe has so much integrity, I am confident he would never have given Ms. Amelia the time of day if he didn't believe her. Yet at the same time, I'm in agony trying to think of a way to clear her name myself, because clearly, no one has paid any attention to her or Gabe after all these years. *Even if I do find the answers needed to exonerate her, how will anyone believe me?*

If I do find clues, they most likely would have been placed there by someone, and why would they try planting "new" old evidence now? As all of these questions and feelings of hopelessness at the monumental task now placed on my shoulders hit me, I feel the tears. They begin running down my cheeks as I watch London somberly handcuff a quiet and stoic Ms. Amelia and assists her to the patrol car.

She pauses at the car door, turns around to me, and with a crack in her voice declares, "Megan, please see that my estate is securely locked up. We'll chat soon, my dear!"

I nod, trying to smile, but only manage replying with a simple, "Okay."

London glances at me with sadness in his eyes, as if trying to somehow say, *I wish I wasn't doing this, Megan.*

Like the sun beginning its slow descent for the night, I allow my tears to fall as I watch London drive away with Ms. Amelia in the back of the patrol car. I suddenly feel lost and defeated, as if I've already let her down and that no matter what I do it won't be enough. I suddenly feel the urge to lock up her estate as quickly as possible. I look into the sky, hoping that by doing so I will find answers or my "writing on the wall."

I walk into the house and secure the front entrance. Then, I head straight to the back-patio area, immediately securing it just as I'd been shown. I look toward the sky in awe. I do not find my answers written there, but I do see a heavenly sunset, so clear and breathtaking. I have to pause! It feels so close, like a mural on a wall that I can reach out and touch. Or a scene in a painting where your heart yearns to get lost within it. Such deep vivid colors; it looks as if the artist pulled each color from the red section of the color wheel and blended them all for tonight's perfect display! I am in awe. It's as if a watercolor of the deepest, most vivid paints has been splashed across the sky, with long sweeping brush strokes that seem to never end. With so many different hues of reds, the detail and brightness in the sky holds me captive. It is stunning and peaceful.

In this divine moment, I understand why her house sits on the property the way it does. Ms. Amelia loves sunsets, and the back-patio garden is the perfect spot to watch each majestic one! Looking around, I begin noticing how the gardener she'd commissioned had strategically placed each of the trees and shrubs in such a way that they frame the sun setting in the western sky. I can see and feel everything come together in one breathtaking picture. The luscious shrubs of lavender, raising their arms to the sky to greet the moon with their soothing aroma. The mighty quaking aspen trees sway in the cool evening breeze, lulling one to sleep with the melodious sound of their leaves, as they dutifully stand guard. The succulent plants and flowers with their beautiful foliage during the day protecting closed buds that bloom into aromatic flowers waking to greet the moon.

I simply can't help myself. Taking off my shoes, I step barefoot onto the soft plush grass, and begin roaming a little as I recognize many of the fragrant flowers: moonflower, evening primrose, queen of the night, four o'clocks, angel trumpets, night scented orchids… I now understand why these were planted close to the seating area. What a heavenly aroma they all make! They are all so perfectly placed throughout the garden, creating a fragrant arousal for the senses! It is so tranquil, so relaxing; I know if I close my eyes, I will fall asleep, so I don't dare. Ms. Amelia and her gardener have created two gardens in one! Stunning!

When I survey the big picture as a whole… the sunset, her desire for privacy and a safe sanctuary away from it all makes sense. This is her Heaven on Earth! I make a mental note to incorporate this explanation with the reverence it deserves into my tours and home listing. Putting my shoes back on, I still get the feeling I am missing the reason I was drawn out here.

I stare into the sunset until my answer comes. A saying I grew up hearing from my grandmother rushes into my memory, "Red sky at night, sailor's delight. Red sky in the morning, sailors take warning." Could this be my writing in the sky, the answer I am looking for? A peace as gentle as a spring rain washes over me, and all my worries go away as quickly as they'd come. I can't trust this peace to stay within me too long. I must run through Ms. Amelia's house and make sure it is locked up. Since I'm here, I'm going to follow in Ms. Amelia's footsteps and make use of her beloved numbers. I send a group text to London and Mona.

Hey guys, I now have seven minutes left at Ms. Amelia's house. I'm currently making sure everything is locked up tight. Please reassure her of this. I'll text you both the instant I'm driving away!

I also need to drive straight to my house as soon as I finish here, since Gabe and his wife are coming by to introduce their dog Ralph to my home while we chat, in preparation for my weekend of dog sitting.

Ignoring both my feelings of being safe and my desire to gaze at the glorious sunset longer, I dart back inside the house. Running straight to the big front doors, I check to make sure they are, in fact, locked. I beeline to the back-patio doors, making sure everything is secure. I scurry around the entire main floor like a mouse, darting to any place where there are windows or doors, any spot that I remember could be used as an exit. Finally, one glance at the security panel and I see it's activated. Before running off, I take a picture of the panel. I'm not sure why, but at this point, I'm not taking any chances. Everything is now tightly locked, all lights off, shades drawn, when a weird thought comes to me, almost audible. *You have a few minutes left, Megan, go upstairs with a fresh set of eyes and look around again.* I race upstairs, saving the master bedroom for last.

Remembering none of the windows upstairs had been touched during our tour, I make quick work of checking the bedroom windows anyway, finally finishing in the master bedroom. I pause at the door, pretending Sherlock Holmes is with me. *What would Sherlock and Watson do?* Always thinking of the practical first, they would most likely investigate anything that felt or looked off or out of the ordinary. Once those were out of the way, they'd move on, seeking the crazy, outside of the box details that, to most, would seem preposterous.

I head straight to the side table I had noticed earlier in the day. I reach into my bag, pulling two tissues out, one for each hand. Using them so as not to leave fingerprints, I pull the unshut drawer all the way out and set it on the floor. Then, I snap some pictures on my phone like I see investigators do in the crime shows on TV. With one of my tissues, I carefully run my hand inside the now empty area, inching my way into the back while praying I find something. I close my eyes and concentrate on what I'm feeling. *Oh, hold on, yes...bingo! It feels like cardstock. Now, if I can just get it out.*

Just as I give it a light tug, I hear what sounds like the tearing of paper. Holding my breath, I readjust my technique and grip so I can try to remove the piece of paper fully intact. Finally, the paper breaks free! I exhale, and to my utter shock realize that I have found a letter. I am sure this is the missing piece of Ms. Amelia's nightmare, the one that could clear her name! As I inspect what I'm holding, I see that I have two pieces of paper, but I'm not sure what the other piece means. It looks like a receipt of sorts, and I am hoping it will prove helpful.

I take a picture of what I've just found, grateful for cell phones that log the time and date of pictures. Returning the drawer to the nightstand, I decide to reach with the tissue into the far back for one last sweep. I pull out a handwritten receipt... *What the ...?!* I take my phone to get another picture and as I do, the clock changes. 7:07 p.m. *Coincidence? I think not!*

Still wondering if I can fully trust London, I text Gabe: *I just found some clues at Ms. Amelia's house!* Then to London, Gabe, and Mona I text: *Just now heading back downstairs at the estate after checking everything is locked before heading out to my car to leave.*

I wrap my findings in a tissue and place them in my bag. I look around quickly, making sure everything is exactly the way I found it. Racing down stairs I pause, closing my eyes and listening to the silence of my surroundings. There is no way I am racing outside with my guard down. I never know who might be watching, hiding or waiting. Using another tissue to press the buttons, I look at the cameras on the security panel, quickly scrolling and skimming through each area on the estate. Once I feel everything is clear, I follow the instructions Ms. Amelia had given me for the security panel before leaving. Keys and bag in hand with nerves on end, I leave.

Time ticks by slowly as I walk over to my car. I hear nothing but the birds chirping their songs. Scanning the front and looking up into the trees, I don't see anyone or anything out of the ordinary, so I start my car saying prayers inside my head, I use voice to text and send an official, "Leaving the estate right now," text to London.

Seconds later he replies. "I forwarded your message to Gabe and the officer on your street so they know to expect you soon." He follows this with a picture of the officer. I finally exhale as I turn onto the main road that heads back into town. Glancing into my rearview mirror, I make sure I am not being followed like last time, and I caution myself to not get excited about what I found.

The breathtaking sunset I'd witnessed earlier returns to the forefront of my mind, and I start thinking of all the metaphors sunsets provide regarding life. Sunsets give us pause, signaling to us our current day is coming to an end. They remind us that even if everything else in our day has gone wrong, we still can choose to go to bed with a peaceful smile on our face, while feeling grateful for one good thing in our day. They remind us we have the opportunity for a new day, which is coming on the horizon, and we can choose to let that promise of tomorrow give us hope. Sunsets can remind us that endings can be beautiful, too. They must be part of what has kept Ms. Amelia going all these years. The promise of a better tomorrow, even when she felt lost and alone! Like the warmth of each color within the sunset I witnessed, so I feel a warmth and reassurance in my soul that maybe Ms. Amelia can be saved with my help after all.

More questions sneak into my mind, breaking my peaceful musings. *What would possess someone to ignore all facts, and continue seeking to indict one particular person? How can people, blindly and without conscience, try to convict a person? Bad things happen when you continue ignoring the truth and you seek to cover it up or silence it.*

Recalling Ms. Amelia's court story, I am reminded of something Sherlock Holmes said in: *A Scandal in Bohemia,* "It's a capital mistake to theorize before one has data. Insensibly, one begins to twist facts to suit theories, instead of theories to suit facts."

Someone's hatred must be the fuel in Ms. Amelia's case, but of what? And this very quote will soon be their demise. We have a good idea of the people who may be responsible, we simply need to catch them! With renewed zest and vigor, I turn onto my street, with all the confidence of renewed zest and vigor that we can get to the bottom of this! I get a glimpse of the officer on patrol. I also see Gabe and his wife pull into my driveway just as my garage door goes up. *Thank God for perfect timing!*

The second my car is in the garage I hit the button to close the door, I heave a sigh of relief. The three of us plus the dog Ralph, are standing by my car. Gabe gallantly opens the door to the kitchen for his wife, Ralph, and me. Gabe and Ralph make quick work of checking to be sure my house is safe. I hear Gabe talking to Ralph upstairs, as his wife and I head into the kitchen. I'd previously met Angelica, at the coffee shop, where Gabe had mentioned he was keeping her informed so that when we talked about it all tonight, nothing would be awkward.

"Angelica, may I offer you some iced tea?" I am so nervous, I don't know what to do with myself. Her sudden smile instantly calms my pounding heart.

"Yes, please, that would be lovely."

Gabe comes to join us, just as I serve the tea. Still a little nervous I sit, awkwardly holding my glass. Angelica opens the conversation and gets straight to the point. "So, darling, Gabe read me your texts. We're both so excited and can't wait any longer to learn what you found at Amelia's!"

I glance over at Gabe and he nods. I tell them everything

in hushed tones even though I know it's only us and the dog. Retrieving my phone, I show them my pictures, leaving nothing out. Everything about the afternoon and evening and what I found at Ms. Amelia's comes tumbling out. "Gabe, what should I do?"

He sits quietly, contemplating his answer, while I'm wondering if I can trust London. *One thing I'm confident about is that my current facial expression gives away exactly how I feel and what I'm thinking. Gabe is sitting so quietly I wonder if he is praying or has suddenly fallen asleep?*

He looks up, takes a drink of tea, and his face relaxes into a pleasant grin. "Megan, I believe you should take all of this to London tomorrow morning. I did wonder why he was absent from the group text, but now I understand your hesitation in doing so. I wish I could be there with you at that time, but we must have faith that everything happens for a reason, whether we like it or not. I'm confident you'll be brave and handle it all just fine. We must trust that it is for the best."

I relax my shoulders as Gabe gives me a winning grin and Angelica reaches over to squeeze my hand.

Gabe continues. "Of course, we'll be praying for you. Goodness knows all this evidence has to show *something*! For years we've agonized over both cases - both the missing painting and the death of that poor girl. Deep within our hearts we've always known Amelia couldn't have committed either of the crimes they say she did, even though the town was convinced she had. It's comforting to know that everyone who played parts in the first two trials has retired, passed on, or moved away. I pray Amelia will now be granted a fair and just trial. Let's just hope the person or persons responsible are still alive and can be brought to justice!"

Feeling a renewed sense of bravery, I ask, "Gabe, do you think I should send my findings to London straight away, rather than waiting till tomorrow?"

He furrows his brows as he ponders both options. "No, I don't think you should, Megan. See, timing is literally everything right now, not to mention our greatest ally. I think you were very smart in handling everything this afternoon with sheer bravery. It was utter genius of you to switch up our meeting time and pick this spot in your house to discuss these pictures. No one will think we are doing anything other than introducing you and Ralph here. Relax, Megan, this evening was impeccable! Thanks to you, I've got a feeling it's all falling into place!"

Gabe and Angelica let me know how they think I should present the pictures to London tomorrow morning. I send a group text letting Gabe, Mona, and London know I'll arrive at the police station promptly at 7:00 in the morning to meet with London about things I'd found at the estate.

We wait, almost not breathing, praying London replies while Gabe and Angelica are still with me. Just as Gabe opens his mouth to say something, we all jump when my phone pings! Laughing, I pull up the text and read the text aloud, "Very interesting, Megan! Excellent detective work! When you pull up, I'll be waiting at the front doors myself. I'll see that your car isn't towed. See you at 7!"

Gabe and his wife stand to leave. "Megan, thank you so much for watching Ralphie for us while we're away. He does seem to like it here - he's already made himself at home at your feet! - and my heart is happy knowing he has you and won't be locked up at a boarding kennel." Ralph looks up at me and nudges my leg with his nose as she says this.

Angelica pulls me into a hug. I shake Gabe's hand and he winks at me. Smiling, I intuitively know our plan is going well. I see them to the door and turn on the porch light. "Good night, you two. Have a lovely trip!"

"Thank you, we will! Be back soon," Angelica calls out as they walk to their car parked in my driveway.

"Ralph, you know what you're to do," Gabe says, lovingly patting Ralph's head.

Ralph gives a short bark in response, wagging his tail. *Ralph does know.* I lock the screen door, followed by the front door, and then turn off the front porch light. Ralph sits back with his ears perked up, intently watching me. His seriousness and pose make me chuckle. "Ralphie, you know exactly what's going on, don't you, boy?" His tail thumps the floor and I swear he winks at me. "Well then, let's be going upstairs! Operation Save Ms. Amelia begins tomorrow, and we must be ready!"

Instead of following me, Ralph goes to the kitchen. "What is it, boy?" He paws at my phone and work bag, then looks at me, tilting his head, curious as to why everything has spilled out. "Brilliant, Ralphie, good boy!" I scoop everything back into my bag with one hand, as I ruffle Ralph's head with the other. After checking to make sure the door leading to the garage is locked, with my bag in hand and Ralph behind me, we go upstairs. I set the burglar alarm, my alarm for 6 a.m., climb into bed, and turn out the light. Ralph lays himself at the door and beats me to sleep.

Morning finds me surprisingly calm. I feel like I finally got a night of solid sleep. As I go through my morning routine, Ralph doesn't let me out of his sight. He stands guard at the top of the stairs until I'm ready to go down. He pads down first and sits patiently at the back door, waiting for me to let him out into the back yard. I look at the security camera that's on the outside of my home, then let Ralph outside. By the time he's ready to come back in, I have his food and water ready, my coffee brewing, my bag ready to go, and Mona has sent me a text letting me know all is clear.

"Well, Ralphie, it's showtime. See you soon!"

I pull up to the police station at exactly seven. London comes out and protectively escorts me in. I open my mouth to speak, but he shakes his head. I'm practically running to keep up, as he ushers me into a small sound-proof room and shuts the door. I sit down catching my breath as he offers me a bottle of water.

"Megan, show me what you've found!"

I tell London everything that happened at the estate after he left with Ms. Amelia. As I carefully pull out the tissue that holds my findings. London nods and jots down notes. He slowly opens the tissue and gasps when he sees what I've handed him.

"Megan, according to all my research on this case plus Gabe's detailed accounts of the first two trials and their evidence, I believe someone has planted this in Ms. Amelia's master bedroom in a desperate attempt to..." He pauses, searching for the right words. "Well," he chuckles, "to be quite honest, I'm not sure to do what."

We both laugh nervously. I'm quick to point out that the receipt may be tied to the stolen painting. He nods in agreement. Then, before he can speak, I feel the strangest urge to spill all of the questions I've been asking about this entire case and every thought I have pondered. So I do. The words and questions just come spilling out. Poor London! I don't know how he can keep up! It's like I can't talk fast enough.

Not phased, London is feverishly taking notes. I don't stop until my heart and mind feel clear. I take a drink of my water while London gets up and starts pacing the floor, hands clasped behind his back deep in thought. "Okay, so obviously these papers must be dusted for fingerprints, before anything else."

I nod in agreement. "You were smart in handling them the way you did, Megan. Thank you, and well done."

"Thank you, London."

"And your questions and observations are sheer genius!"

"Oh!" I breathlessly manage. I start feeling antsy watching him pace. "London, why don't I show you the pictures I took after you and Ms. Amelia left? Maybe they'll help you."

"Right. Okay, then, let's have a look at 'em," he says pulling a chair around to sit next to me.

My heart rate slows as I exhale. "Here they are," I say, handing him my phone. I wait with bated breath. In my mind I had pictured a calm London looking through my pictures, pinching the screen to enlarge some of the photos, and maybe asking me a few questions. Instead, I am jolted from my peace.

"Megan! These are perfect!!!" he shouts as he knocks over his chair, leaping from his seat to bolt out of the room with my phone in hand! Then he runs back in and closes the door behind him.

"Megan, I'm sorry. Do you give verbal consent for me to take your phone and have copies of these pictures made? I'll bring the papers for you to sign immediately after I take this to the lab. They need to go to forensics!"

Giggling, half from fright and half because he looks so out of character, giddy with excitement, I give verbal consent.

"Thank you! I'll be right back." He is practically squealing like a little kid at Christmas time.

I'm not sure how long I've been in this room now waiting for London to return. In a way, it gives me time to think over my life since arriving in Alton Rose. Now that I've spilled everything about this case, there's not much more to think about. All I really wanted to do was help people and families find their perfect home, yet the moment I stepped into the office, I was thrown into detective work against my will. However, despite unsettling feelings and a bit of fear, I'm the first to admit it has turned out to be exciting and rewarding in many ways! I'm still learning to recognize and acknowledge my inner confidence, but I guess that's also a continued journey of the soul that takes time. I know I felt much more confident and grounded this time coming into the police station.

I'm also feeling grateful my position has allowed me to do all of this - the unexpected detective work blended seamlessly with prepping Ms. Amelia's home for sale. After looking back, I fear that if I'd been given the opportunity to choose involvement or not, this entire situation would've played out quite differently.

I think of how I handled the mysterious side of my client. In hindsight, she was smart in picking me to sell her home, as I hadn't had the chance to be influenced by the town's opinion of her. So, by not knowing her and the situation, I was able to see her as a soul in need of a friend and the perfect person to sell her estate. I cannot think of anything I regret.

I'm relieved I can finally sit and process all of this from beginning to end. I haven't really been able to until now.

My mind jumps to Ms. Amelia still locked in a jail cell somewhere in this building. *I'm so worried about her and the estate with no one there. Oh sure, the cameras are on and everything is locked tight. But, still...* I sigh, reaching for my phone, before realizing I don't have it. If I did, I could text Mona. *Oh well, at least she knows where I am.*

I sit staring at the blank wall in front of me, wondering about John's crazy behavior a few nights ago in the foyer. I realize I'd not found a reason or solution for this and now that my mind is clear it's popped back in, wanting resolution. *John always seemed so astute and put together, so refined and genteel, never seeming forgetful...ever! I'm still puzzled why he decided to go out into the garden that evening, especially when Ms. Amelia has a gardener...unless...NO WAY! I remember seeing a list for the gardener on her table when we were in her hidden tower room. Wait a minute...hang on! Well, actually, is it possible? Oh geez, does Ms. Amelia know? No she doesn't, given the confused expression on her face regarding John's behavior, she couldn't possibly have known.*

And, given her reaction when she counted...My mind is coming up with the next thought before I've even finished the last. A mile a minute doesn't do it justice and I need to get this to London NOW!

Well, hopefully Ms. Amelia doesn't know what I'm pretty sure I've just unraveled! Oh, this is huge! I really need to tell London what I've just figured out, and talk him through step by step! *Come on, why can't London hurry up?!* Just when I thinkI've been forgotten, London runs in waving the papers he needs me to sign.

I feverishly sign the papers as London catches his breath. "London, you sure are excited about something!" I can't control myself and let out a sly remark about his lack of composure.

"You will be too, Megan, when you see who got caught in one of your pictures! Boy, oh boy, is Gabe gonna be proud of you!? I mean, he'll be jealous he didn't figure it out, but also super proud of you at the same time! Oh, I can't wait to see the look on his face!" He can barely contain his excitement and I can't tell if he's more excited about what we've found or that we found it before Gabe.

By now, I'm just as excited as London, and still a little annoyed that he isn't giving it up. The suspense is killing me! Almost as if reading my thoughts, London regains his composure and practically whispers a plan.

"Megan, I want to tell you so badly, I really do! But walls have ears and I can't risk you and your safety any further if anything gets out. Plus, there are protocols I need to follow and I need to follow through on some paperwork and technicalities before I can tell you any more. I'll be sending my partner, Allen, with you as you leave. He's waiting for you at the front desk. When you see him, smile, say good-bye, and act nonchalant as you leave. He'll follow you back to your office and you'll park just like you normally do. He'll go around the block a few times and get coffee, you know...his normal morning patrol routine. Then, he'll double back to pick up you and Mona and drive you both to the estate. Once people see a cop car, they'll assume a lot of things about Ms. Amelia, and many others will have their guard down. Then, BAM!"

I jump. "Jeez Louise, London! But, you still haven't really explained yourself."

"Megan, all the questions you've been asking are brilliant and observational, and I'm so happy Amelia told you everything in the way that she did! Her case has been used in the past as an educational tool, because none of us want to ever have a cold case like this. We strive for swift and accurate justice, open and shut cases, and this one has puzzled so many of us for years. I hope and pray our plan works!"

"Wow. Okay, London, and thank you. Umm, I have another question."

"Yes, Megan?"

"I'm dying to know; when will you tell me who you think did it or who it was that was in one of my pictures?"

"Megan, I will call you back to the police station for further questioning tomorrow after lunch. Then, as soon as I am able, I promise I will tell you."

I nod, getting up to leave. London hands me my phone.

"Now, Megan, you remember what's next, right?"

"I do. May I leave now? I really need to get to the office." I glance at my phone to see nine texts from Mona, a message from a client, and one from Gabe. He nods, so I grab my bag and put on my acting face. Not trusting the emotions that may be spread across my face, I do my best to act brave and head out of the meeting room.

Chapter 13

*"Education never ends Watson. It is a series of lessons,
with the greatest for the last."*

-Sherlock Holmes, His Last Bow

The morning unfolds just as London said it would. Mona and I, along with our home stager, make quick work of the pictures I'd taken at the estate, labeling each picture, plus marking some pieces of furniture in each room that need to be packed up. I've already checked, and London and his team have copied many of the photos that might be evidence. I'm guessing he's made a copy of these, too. We have fun occupying our time planning and keeping ourselves distracted by using a special photo editing app that allows you to move things around or delete items in rooms that you have pictures of.

We start with the pictures of the kids' rooms first, then tackle the kitchen pictures since they were the easiest. The secret tower room, chapel, and butler's pantry quickly pass inspection by our stager. For the downstairs library, we decide to leave most of the books in place and pack all the photos and travel memorabilia. This will free up quite a few shelves, allowing a simple vase or another art piece in the room to sit alone, giving it a modern, clutter-free look almost instantly.

While Mona is making a few calls and our stager heads out to another project, I pull out all of the boxes, tape, and Sharpies that Mona had been collecting over the last few days. I am grateful our stager understands this situation and we can trust her to be confidential. She, of course, would come through at the very end, but at this stage in the process, there is really no need for an extra person. With our pictures now saved, we print out the new rooms, so we know exactly what to do in each. This will make everyone's life easier. *I just hope we've deleted the correct items out of each room.*

I wonder if I can visit Ms. Amelia in jail? Surely, she won't be in there too long, right? I'm pretty confident I have identified all the items needing to be packed up, but I could do with Ms. Amelia double checking. I'd hate for anything to get accidentally left behind and end up getting stolen.

For the next few hours, Mona and I find random jobs to occupy our time. Setting everything we need by the front entrance, packing our work bags, rearranging the new office furniture...

London's partner, Allen, finally arrives and it's showtime! As we sit in his police car heading to the estate, I allow myself to reflect on my carefree morning. I think through what should happen at the estate today. *So far, everything is going just the way London said it would. Allen looks deep in thought.*

"Megan, I'd like to make myself useful in each room and help you two in any way I can. That'll give me the opportunity to look around the house. To be honest, I'm quite curious about this place I've heard so much about but never seen, and I can also get to you quickly if needed. How does this sound to you both?"

"I think that's a brilliant idea, Allen! If you have any questions, please feel free to ask them. We *must* get this nightmare figured out for Ms. Amelia, no matter what!"

He agrees with me.

As we park in front of the house, I swear I see someone behind a tree. Something shifts into the shadows, and I reassuringly tell myself I must be jittery. But, Allen must have seen it too, because he barely gets the car into park before he jumps out and takes off running in that direction.

Mona and I hurriedly load our arms with everything so we only have to make one trip inside. We hold our breath as I reset the alarm. Lately, Ms. Amelia has been keeping the security recordings going, so I replay the few minutes till it catches up to real time...sure enough, there is the creepy guy from the library!! *Oh, sweet football tackle from Allen!* He takes him down and hand-cuffs him.

A few minutes later, his sirens are blaring. Allen texts that he's taking the guy in for questioning, hopefully charging him with trespassing, and he'll be back later. Mona and I waste no time running upstairs to start work on the kids' rooms. Mona stares wide eyed with amazement as I had when I first saw them. Smiling to myself, I let her look around while I ready some boxes and label them. In no time flat we finish the boys' room and have the boxes stacked neatly near the door. While Mona is vacuuming, I walk over to Ms. Amelia's daughter's room and prepare the boxes in there. Mona scurries over, and we give this room as much zealousness as the first.

I find out that Mona loves to vacuum, so while she's finishing up, I run into the chapel and dust. From down the hallway I hear Mona scream! Running in with my camera on record, I find her staring at a family photo and pointing. "He. He. He, that's... but why?"

"Mona, please breathe with me. Take some deep breaths. We're safe. Please come sit down." I knew who it was she'd seen in one of the pictures, Amelia's first husband. Having no choice, I find myself giving her a three-minute synopsis of Ms. Amelia's life story.

Mona finally looks up at me. "Megan, I've seen this guy lurking around town, and I just *know* he's the guy that broke into our office!"

"No, Mona, I didn't know. Are you sure?" I can tell by her reaction though that she is absolutely sure. "Deep breaths, Mona, deep breaths."

I can see Mona is calming down. This is good, because it gives her a chance to process all she's heard and seen. "Mona, you're gonna have more questions, so I'll be right here packing boxes. Feel free to simply ask." *I know we could sit and dwell on this far too long, but she'll just have to trust me, given the fact that time is not on our side.*

Mona sits quietly, trying to calm down even more, and soon begins asking me questions. With this, I feel my own anxiety beginning to rise. I soon realize Mona is wanting the whole story, and we are only in the second bedroom! To be fair, I do understand where she is coming from - this mystery has been going on for so long and there are so many unanswered questions. I groan inwardly and on the outside begin pleading with her.

"Mona, we don't have time for Ms. Amelia's entire backstory right now, because, believe me it's a doozy. You're just going to have to trust me and wait until we're heading back into town."

Closing my eyes, I breathe in deeply, while praying this answer can be enough, and go back to packing boxes. I look over and realize Mona isn't going to be much help, as she's still looking at the pictures.

"Mona, please," I beg in exasperation. "I'm not trying to be mean or pushy, but you can't sit there the whole time. Literally every second we have here counts!"

Finally she snaps out of it. "I'm sorry, Megan. I'm just beginning to understand so much now. I know bits and pieces of Amelia's story and now I just have a ton of questions."

"Yeah, you're telling me! Join the club." *If you only knew, Mona.* "Welcome to my life since my first day on the job. I've had a million and one questions still waiting for answers and didn't even know any of her story before!"

Mona looks to protest, and then thinks better of it. We go

back to packing boxes in silence. Every noise makes us jump and our nerves are on edge. While Mona begins stacking the packed boxes near the door, I start preparing the boxes we'll need for the master bedroom, and share little snippets of my excitement from the last two days. Mona interjects every now and then with information she's discussed with London or pieces of knowledge she's heard over the years. Most of what she says I already know, but it's nice to pass the time chatting. It takes our mind off of what we're actually wondering: *Where on earth is Allen?!* I help stack the last few boxes by the bedroom door.

Soon, Mona is back to her bubbly self. Laughing and racing downstairs to the dining room, we freeze at the sound of a car's engine and crunching gravel.

"Please let it be Allen," Mona prays.

I hand Mona the box I was taping and run into the kitchen to look at the security camera. "Mona, I can't find a car in any of the screenshots!"

"Keep looking, Megan! How a car drove onto this property without buzzing the gate is beyond me. But that was most definitely a car we just heard. While I'm in here I'm going to go ahead and start wrapping up some of Ms. Amelia's china - we need to hustle before whoever that is gets here."

I keep looking through footage. Three minutes later I find it. "Gotcha!" I squeal.

Mona runs in. "Who, Megan, who?!"

"I'm not sure, but I have a car," I answer, whipping out my phone to take a picture of the security screen. "Mona, I need you to continue clicking this button until you see a human. I'm going to send this picture to London, tell him what happened, and have him send Allen and extra back-up to the estate."

"Great think...Meg-g-gan...oh, dear Jesus!"

My heart almost stops. I spin around to look at the screen and completely freeze. There's Anita, looking as if she's searching for something she's dropped on the ground.

"Hurry, Megan, take a picture!" Mona screams, her voice slapping me back to reality. "Do you know how to record on this system? Oh my goodness, is it recording?!? What are we going to do?"

I frantically snap a picture. I wonder what Anita is looking for. *And, why the heck is she here???* The way she's searching makes it seem as if she's been here before and now is hunting for something she noticed went missing. *But, how in the world did she make it onto the property without using the gate?*

I send both pictures to London with as urgent a text as possible:

Send backup with Allen ASAP

To catch Anita

CANNOT use sirens!

I somehow manage to hit a button on the security panel that sends the last hour of footage to the police station! *Who knew such a thing existed! What a convenience!* Realizing what I'd just done, I race my texts with another one, stating my newest discovery was sent to the police station, just as the front door-knob starts rattling.

This is great! Mona and I are going to die at the hands of Anita or die of a heart attack right here in the middle of Ms. Amelia's kitchen! Something possesses me to look at the clock. Miracles never cease. It's exactly 3:03 in the afternoon! In that instant, I know it's all going to be okay. I don't know how, I don't know why, I just know it's all going to work out. I glance down at my phone. London has texted saying he, Allen, and back-up are on their way, and to not let anyone in.

As we sneak into the dining room, I read Mona the text I got from London. Thankfully the curtains had been drawn, the door to the foyer was already closed, and the door leading back into the kitchen had conveniently swung shut behind us, leaving us completely out of view from any prying eyes from the patio doors. Now, we just need to remain quiet no matter what. I make sure my phone is on silent and motion to Mona to do the same.

Mona shows me the texts she sent to London, letting him know where we are and asking him to text us when they arrive at the gate. She then frantically messages that Anita is trying to get in, and that it sounds like she's trying to pick the lock on the front door. *Doesn't this woman have any idea about the security systems???* London lets Mona know they are barreling down the road now, with their lights flashing but no sirens. She holds her phone up so I can see the next message from him saying,

Baby, don't worry, we'll turn the lights off as we get to Ms. Amelia's road. I just want you to be safe. XXX And, Megan, too.

I wink at Mona and nod toward the phone so she knows to look at the latest message.

Satisfied, we look around. Our eyes have adjusted to the late afternoon light, so we quietly begin boxing up what we know must go. Time is of the essence, and we need to keep ourselves occupied. Somehow, someway. I open the lower doors on the buffet and find cloth storage boxes for plates. Just as I finish clearing off the settings on the table, a huge electrical zap sounds and buzzes through the air, followed by a woman's scream. Shaking and frightened, both of us want to find out what's going on, but we don't dare do anything that would signal we are here... *Oh, no! The screens in the windows!*

Mona is shaking so hard, she lays her phone on the table and tries texting London what has just happened, but her fingers can barely find the right letters. I go back to packing out of necessity, and partly out of my desire to focus on anything other than possibly getting killed.

"Megan, did you hear that?"

"Hear what?"

"That voice, it's calling for someone. Can you make out a name or anything? Did you hear it? There it is again!" she exclaims in a whisper.

I muffle my sudden and inexplicable laughter, snorting instead.

"Megan, how in the name of sanity can you be laughing right now?" Mona asks in an exasperated whisper.

All I can do is shrug my shoulders, since I don't want to start laughing out loud. Once I let go, I know I won't stop. I can't help but hear it, too, and I too am terrified, despite my uncontrollable laughter. *Maybe I'm laughing at the thought of karma finally catching up to the shadow that has haunted Ms. Amelia for so long and can't contain my excitement.*

Shaking, I manage to open the camera and hit record, moving around the room slowly so I can find where the voice is the loudest. I have an idea where it's coming from, but want to be sure. Bingo! The voice sends chills down my spine. Mona and I are on the verge of tears, it's so creepy. Clearly the person who fell is not doing well, sounds older, and seems to be injured in some way. I continue recording, and am grateful that I only need sound, as I am still shaking.

Mona comes over and grabs onto me. There is that eerie voice again. It just won't stop. I glance down at my phone, making sure it's still recording.

"Help-p-p-p me. Wha-wha where...are you? Why weren't you in the house? I kn-kn-knew we shouldn't have come b-b-back h-h-here! Mmmaybe you found the money."

Suddenly the realization of the sad state she is in hits me. Slouching my shoulders forward, I fall into a dining room chair ruminating on what I'd just put together in my mind. *Oh Anita, why did you let hate consume you? You have ruined so many lives because of this! What on earth were you trying to prove? Ms. Amelia was nothing but kind to you. She couldn't control the acci-*

dent that killed your husband on the estate, and it was very un-
fortunate that he died. I can only imagine the pain of losing your
husband. But, she and Luther never hid what happened, and they
honored your late husband by taking financial care and settling
things for you. Out of the three widows, you have never been able to
let it go, you've run her through the mud instead, and it was never
her fault to begin with. Your daughter died because of you. Was all of
your guilt too much for you?

The mixed emotions I am feeling are too much, as I
realize what most likely lies in store for her soon. I assume Ms.
Amelia's window security is still working quite well and that
when Anita tried opening a window, she received a shock causing her to be thrown backwards to the ground.

Finally, the security speaker rings. Knowing our tres-
passer, Anita, is on the side of the house, I race into the kitchen.
"H-h-hi." My voice is filled with a gamut of unprocessed emotions.

"It's London. We're all here. Are you ladies okay?"

"Yes, and I hope you have at least two squad cars! Anita,
tried breaking in one of the windows, and is lying on the side of
the house suffering from an electrical shock. I also have her on a
recording. I think she was calling out, believing she was talking
to the creepy guy from the library. OH! And guess what?!? There
is another entrance somewhere on the estate! Oh - and get an
ambulance here for Anita, and quick!"

My quick thinking and resourcefulness kicks in. Without
overthinking, I take action and I am going with it. There's no
time to wait for anyone else to step in.

The buzzer sounds, letting me know I've pressed the correct button, and the entrance gate is now swinging open.

I hope something I've come across over these past few weeks
will free Ms. Amelia...somehow. Now, it's left up to the police to
sort out. I must hold on to some hope for Ms. Amelia, though, since

they will definitely be reopening the case. I know this time, whatever happens she has me, and hopefully Gabe, to proudly stand beside her. I am sure the town will go crazy again. The police will need to interview everyone again. I should save the recording so London has as close to a confession as possible. Who was it that said timing is everything?

I'm jolted out of my thoughts by loud banging on the door, London's bellowing voice, and loud orders being screamed outside. I grab the final box and place it inside the server. In spite of everything, Mona and I have somehow managed to finish in the dining room, and for that, my heart is grateful. She grabs my hand and we run to the door, barely getting it unlocked as London and Allen excitedly barge in, slamming the door back looking like they are ready for war.

I can't help but giggle.

Since laughter is contagious and a much better emotion to handle what we've just come through, Mona tries stifling her own laugh, managing to say, "At ease soldiers!"

At the sudden realization of how they'd just barged in, London and Allen start laughing. Once they start laughing, I can no longer hold back my own, and soon all four of us become a laughing mess. The shrill sirens on the ambulance out front stop our laughter, and we collapse onto the foyer floor. I didn't realize until just now how my body was craving a moment to sit down.

Someone'ss walkie-talkie beeps. "Sir, we're leaving with the suspect. We'll follow the ambulance to the hospital, the paramedics say she should be okay."

London's face gets stern. "Yes! Stay with her until further notice. I don't want her out of your sight."

"Yes, sir! Over and out."

We all sit staring at the floor waiting for our adrenaline to regulate and not quite sure what to do next. I know what questions I need to ask, but I don't know if London will answer them. I'm getting antsy knowing Ms. Amelia and John are locked up, and there's still so much to do here at the estate. I have to leave soon because I never made it home during lunch hour to let Ralph out; poor buddy.

Glancing over at London, it looks as if he's wrestling with something on his mind. I can't hold back any longer. I must ask. I feel I deserve an answer. I open my mouth to speak, but London starts first, so I shut my mouth.

"Megan, I have some news. I was going to share it later, but I guess now is as good a time as any. The letter you found had Anita's figure prints all over it. Basically, she was trying to frame Amelia, again for everything. But, since the letter had Anita's figure prints all over it, it was obvious she had written it. Not to mention, the signature on the letter didn't match Amelia's at all. When we had Anita in for questioning we took a handwriting sample, and the slant to her writing matched the one on the letter. So, we're booking Anita for forgery, and I am only getting started with this woman."

It seems there is a laundry list of offenses they can - and will - pin on Anita.

"After pouring over all the evidence from the first case, plus getting Gabe and the other retired officer's accounts, it is clear the letter was recently placed in the house. Everything you've told me matches and gives Amelia an alibi. She actually wants to stay locked up right now because she feels it would be safer than being at the estate by herself, or alone in a hotel. And, after what has happened today, I can certainly understand her desire to do so. Currently, we are holding the guy from the library under trespassing violations, and John under assisting a crime until we can prove another reason to hold them, but it seems the violations are building up on their own. Time will soon tell us more. There's a new judge, so that helps, but I'm unsure about what will happen next and where the jury may come from. Since you told me of all that Amelia, Gabe, and John have shared with you, everything is starting to make sense and come together like a puzzle. Truth will always come, but sometimes we just need to look harder for it. We have wonderful leads, fresh eyes looking into the case, and Gabe just won't rest until the truth is out. I'd say this is quite a fair start!"

London places a hand on the floor and pushes himself up to stand. "Come on, Allen, let's get these ladies home."

As we lock up before settling into the squad car for the trip back to the office, I get the feeling Ms. Amelia is going to be okay. "London, would it be alright if I take Ms. Amelia her favorite coffee? I want to go over some questions I have before we begin staging at her estate. At least I'd like to because I don't see how we'll ever get her house sold if I can't."

He's about to answer when a very exasperated voice comes across his radio. "London, someone's playing a nasty trick! There are two of them and I don't know who's who! I'm unable to follow through with the release order, sir, because I don't know which man I can free! Over!"

London grips the steering wheel until his knuckles turn white. Panic seeps back onto all of our faces. My only consolation is in remembering that earlier I'd wondered about John having a twin and had shared my thoughts with London back at the police station. Even though he had dismissed it and laughed it off at the time, he did reassure me that, as crazy as this whole case is, he couldn't rule it out. Now, I think he's beginning to see that my hunch is correct!

"Megan, would you like a job working alongside Allen on the investigation unit?" he asks me with a sly grin.

Instead of answering him, I smile and wink. "I guess my hunch was correct then, huh?"

Mona's thoughts get the best of her, "How are you going to tell who's who? Wait, who and what are we talking about?"

We all laugh and London explains that is information

for another day. He winks at me, knowingly. *London really had listened.* Even though it had seemed far-fetched at the time, he had actually paid attention to everything I had said. Mona is nodding and throwing a smile my way. Gosh, it feels good knowing London had trusted me.

As we pull up in front of the office, London answers my earlier question, "I'll see you back at the jail in a half-hour, Megan. Either Allen or I will be waiting for you out front and will take you back to Amelia. To adhere to visitation guidelines within the jail and not risk preferential treatment, I ask that you please keep your visit to an hour max. Be precise, be careful with what you say, and make no small talk. I will quietly and carefully give Amelia the same notification. We're treating her well, Megan. She actually thinks this is fun, God bless her, and has told me much of the same things you said. She's been cute to watch, always calm and dignified, and has whipped a few of the women with attitudes into shape. It's safe to say the entire Alton Rose police department is growing rather fond of her."

Smiling and exhausted, Mona and I sink into the nearest chairs.

I'm finally back into a blissful state of calm, when my to-do list barges to the front of my mind forcing me to accept what I must do, tired or not. I groan.

"Megan, what's the matter?" I glance over at Mona, and she still has her eyes closed.

"Oh, it's just...my mind is reminding me of all I have to do, but there is only one of me."

"Well, may I help? After all," she says with a giggle, "I *am* your Watson!"

"That's a sweet offer, Watson. Thank you." I sit up, finding some reserve of energy I didn't know I had left.

"First, we'll need to lock up here. If you could please swing by my place and let Ralph out to run and do his business,

149

and see he has fresh water and a large scoop of food, I'd be super grateful. While you're doing that, I'll grab coffee, run over to meet with Ms. Amelia, and then go home."

"Certainly, Megan! When did you have time to get a dog? Never mind, you can tell me later. I'll order us some food. How does Chinese sound? The sweetest Asian restaurant just opened up near my apartment. Mmm, it's so fresh, all organic, and yummy. It's a hip new spin on the classics! Something we need in this old little town."

"Sounds perfect, Mona. You know I can't say no to Asian food!" I grab my phone and place my coffee order, then prepare to leave. Mona gets her things together, locks up, and we leave in opposite directions.

When I enter Oswald's Coffee Shop, I see Gabe and the guys at a table in the corner. *Wait! Gabe? Why are they home a day early?* It's like he really is all-knowing, and it doesn't help his case for not being an angel when Gabe turns around with a big grin.

"Megan! My wife and I are home early because I have to be questioned tomorrow since the case has reopened. What brings you into the coffee shop at this hour?"

"Well, Gabe, I was going to ask you the same thing, but it seems we both are here for the same reason," I say, grabbing my coffee order. "It is going to be a long night for me!. When are you stopping by to pick up Ralph? He's been such a wonderful room-mate and guard dog these last few days. I'm going to miss him."

"Awww, I'm so glad to hear Ralphie was such an amazing gentleman. I feel like I should let him stay with you. I'll swing by to pick him up tomorrow as planned."

"Sounds great, Gabe. Nice to see you boys again," I say with a wave.

Back in my car, I text London to let him know I'm on my way. Three blocks later, I pull up to the station to see him waiting with excitement in his eyes.

"Megan, we've just had the biggest breakthrough, but I can't tell you just yet. I'll need you to come in for some more questioning tomorrow. Please, please don't freak out like before. Just answer the questions this time, okay?"

I nod and pass through the scanner and check in. By now I know the protocol and the guards on duty. I follow London quietly as he leads me to the jail. Once cleared for visitation, I sit in a room, while London retrieves Ms. Amelia. Remembering the one hour we have, I jump up and lay out all the staging info and pictures on the table to save a little time. Just as I finish, the door swings open, and a very happy Ms. Amelia walks in. She embraces me in a hug, which I am not expecting, pinning my arms to my side.

"Oh, I'm so happy to see you! London tells me it's all business and straight to the point, so let's go! Oh, and you brought my favorite coffee, too? Megan, you're so sweet! What a needed treat!"

London stands guard at the door.

"As you can see, Ms. Amelia, here are the photos of your home as-is, and in this next pile you'll find edited ones. To stage a home, standard protocol is to remove all items that say "current owner," and reduce clutter, which allows the new buyer to look at it as their own. This way they can see their own belongings in the space more easily. It is this set of pictures here that Mona and I need your approval on."

As she begins looking at the photos, I launch into a quick explanation of the app we used to edit her pictures. By the look on her face, she's quite impressed. "As you can see, the items that have been removed are paintings and objects that are your prized possessions. If you see anything else in the photos you wish to have boxed up and removed, please tell me. I'll get it taken care of. The bedrooms are all finished, and the boxes are labeled and stacked in the rooms ready to go. Since we didn't know whose things were whose in the boys' room, we boxed all their items together, so they'll have to sort those boxes on their own. We made quick work in the dining room as well, so all that's left for me to do tomorrow is tackle the library."

Ms. Amelia nods as she looks over each picture, then smiles. "Megan, excellent work! You removed all the correct items, but there is one place I've not shown you nor told you about."

I snap my head to look at her so quickly, I feel myself getting a headache, or whiplash! "You what?!" I sigh in exasperation. "Ms. Amelia, this is no time for games!"

She calmly takes a generous gulp of her coffee, smiling a mischievous grin. "Don't worry your pretty little self over it, dearie. We never got to it, because we didn't have the chance. It's John's anyway! When you go over there tomorrow, you can see it. You won't have to pack it, though, John can take care of it himself. Basically, it is his home on our lowest level. It is nice and homey down there, maintains an even temperature throughout the year, and you'd never know you were in a basement."

By this time, I have regained control of my facial expressions, my shock has subsided, and I jot down a few notes.

"London told me John should be released tomorrow, so maybe you can be his ride back to the estate?" I look over at London, and he nods in agreement.

"There's no reason to keep him any longer. Megan, be back at the police station at 10 a.m. In keeping with standard protocol, I ask that you stay in your car, and we'll bring John out to you. Amelia will stay here through tomorrow, too, so I'll text you when it's her time to be released, and you'll follow the same protocol so you can collect her as well. Okay, two minutes left ladies. Amelia, finish your coffee please. Also, do you feel good about what Megan and Mona have done with your estate so far?"

She nods, swallowing the last bit of her coffee. "Oh yes, I love it! These gals have done such a lovely job! I can't wait to call my kids and set up a time for them to come see the place, have one last party, and take their boxes!"

Our happy moment is interrupted by static and the exasperated voice of the same cop I'd heard earlier paging London on his radio.

"Ladies, it looks like you're needed to help clear up a situation. Come with me and I'll explain when we get there!"

London leads us into the room used for lineups, explaining our help is needed in figuring out which John is actually Ms. Amelia's butler, and which is John's evil twin. It has become clear that John is clear of charges, and they now need to make sure the right man is in custody.

Ms. Amelia is in absolute shock. I link her arm within mine to give her added support and jog her memory back to the night in the foyer when John was acting strange. A lightbulb moment occurs for her. Nodding, she proceeds to share two other similar instances: once in the garden, and once in the library a few months prior to my arrival in Alton Rose when John had also acted strange.

We step into the mirrored room and Ms. Amelia gasps. Standing in the room are identical twins! In all facial features they look alike, in height and body build they are the same, and dressed in identical drab inmate uniforms. No wonder they were having a hard time telling the two apart! I've seen my share of identical twins before, but these two were exactly alike in every detail. They both also look extremely irritated and miserable!

Completely at a loss for words, Ms. Amelia stares back and forth at them and then looks at London and me. I see this will not get us anywhere fast, and I want to get home to my girls' evening with Mona and eat the delicious Chinese food she ordered for us. My stomach grumbles in anticipation. I squeeze Ms. Amelia's arm pulling it closer to me and holding tight. "Ms. Amelia, can you spot their differences?" *I sure can't.*

She shakes her head no, her eyes pleading for help. *Okay, Sherlock, let's think.* "London, butler John needs a cane to walk properly. Could we have them walk around?"

London asks them to walk around the room. There is hesitancy as both want to begin, but are looking at the other, waiting for the other one to start. *It's like they don't trust each other or one is waiting to copy the other.* I can't tell which one is copying who, because they both end up limping, each limping slightly differently, but I'd never seen our John without his cane.

"Ms. Amelia, have you ever seen John without his cane?"

"No, I haven't."

London is beginning to get irritated. This case seems never-ending. Looking at him, I ask if we could have both men put on the clothes they were wearing when they came in to be booked. Knowing that the true John will have a neat, butler's uniform that smells of sweet European cologne, and the other will have wrinkled clothes that will smell earthy due to hiding amongst the trees outside. One will have a cane within his possessions, and the other won't. I remind London of my observation that night in the foyer.

"Megan, what sheer genius!" Ms. Amelia exclaims joyously.

London nods and exits the room to set this plan in motion.

"I do pray this plan of yours works," Ms. Amelia whispers.

Soon, London rushes back in to let us know that the twins will come at different times, and he will be turning on the mic at a certain point so they can answer a few questions and hopefully end this drama. London presses a buzzer and a cop with big muscles shows up with one of the twins: no cane, in wrinkled street clothes, and slightly limping. London presses the buzzer, and another cop shows up with a proud, dignified, yet tired looking man with a cane and dressed in a pristine butler's uniform.

"JOHN!" Ms. Amelia shouts. Since the speaker is on because no one was expecting the outburst, the real John looks toward the sound of the voice, smiling and waving, and the other looks at his brother with disdain.

Problem solved! I'm ready for my Chinese food!

London decides to let the men stay in their clothes, telling me that after I finish answering questions tomorrow he'll release the real John, as originally planned, to me so I can take him home once I'm out front. I can now go home. Ms. Amelia gives me another unexpected hug, and I practically run out of the police station.

Arriving home, Mona and Ralphie are snuggled up on the couch, and the smell of Chinese food is in the air. Both jump up excited to see me. Ralph and I go around the house, making sure it's locked up tight, while Mona plates our food. In between bites, I recount the last few hours, while Mona listens intently to my every word as if her very breath depends on it. She nearly chokes when my phone goes off, scaring the both of us. London's calling. Mona puts him on speaker.

"Megan, after interrogation and some threatening words, John's brother confessed. He said he'd been called by Luther on behalf of Anita, asking him to spy on Ms. Amelia. After Luther's untimely death, he and Anita remained in contact but he went back home to England, only returning to Alton Rose a few months ago. Apparently, Anita had been thinking Amelia was up to something and asked him to see what he could find out. He's been spying ever since. Well, ladies, enjoy the rest of your evening."

Mona and I each take a few bites of our food, as the realization hits us that Anita's life is about to be turned upside down. And, in all likelihood, Ms. Amelia's too, yet again. Mona tells me all about Anita's second husband and how sweet he was to her and her daughter before she died. "He always spoke so lovingly of them both as his girls. I don't understand how Anita could have hidden all this from him all these years, and I am so grateful he is safe in Heaven resting with one of his girls. At least he'll never have to see his beloved Anita go through trial." She sighs, taking another bite of orange chicken.

The next day at the police station, we finally clear up the mystery behind who Library Guy is: Amelia's ex-husband Hunter! After questioning, it turns out that the receipts Anita had John's twin plant in Ms. Amelia's bed-side table were the receipts from the sale of the painting that had been stolen from the art gallery that fateful night. After some quick thinking by an investigator, the receipts were traced back to Hunter. It was he who had bought the stolen painting from Anita in a quiet sale, then sold it to a museum for a large sum of money. He has been living comfortably off that money ever since.

Anita had promised the proceeds of the sale to him as payment for his spying. Feeling relieved that this time Ms. Amelia's name would in fact be cleared, I eagerly wait in my car for John. I look at my watch and smile. *Hmmm...I wonder if Gabe is at the coffee shop with his friends right now before heading over to the police station?*

I look up to see John with his cane practically bouncing out of the police station. As he gets in the car he blurts out with excitement thick with his English accent, "Well, young lady, this ol' boy is ready for home. Off we go!"

"Wait a minute, John. I have a little surprise for you! And since today is great cause for celebration, I will *not* take no for an answer!" He looks at me puzzled, but flashes me his handsome smile and nods his head.

As soon as we're inside Oswald's coffee shop, John and I are met with loud cheers from the baristas behind the counter, Gabe, and all his buddies. John is practically glowing with pride and emotionally choked up at his hero's welcome. What a delightful time we have! It brings me great joy to see John cutting it up, laughing, and having a great time. Finally, some joy is coming his way. As I take in the raucous scene in front of me, I wonder how long it's been since John has had fun like this, and I'm so glad I followed my heart. He certainly needed this little surprise to end his ordeal.

With our hearts overflowing, we leave the coffee shop and begin the drive to take John home. Turning the car toward the estate, a comfortable silence falls over us in the car. I can sense John wanting to speak, so I invite him. "John, it's just us in the car. You know I have your back, so come on...out with it!"

He chuckles. "I'm trying to figure out where I'm going to put all my possessions. I'm wondering where I'm going to go and what I'm going to do next. If I were to go back to the UK, I wouldn't know what to do with myself. This town is my chosen family and my home. I could go visit my family in England for a time, but I would definitely want to return home to Alton Rose."

"John, remember, you and Ms. Amelia really haven't had time to sit and talk about it, so I wouldn't worry about it just yet. Simply bring up the question tomorrow evening when you can both sit down freely and talk."

"That's quite true indeed. We certainly haven't been free to talk much about anything. Thank you for the sound advice, Megan."

Turning onto Beauregard Lane, I notice John sit up a little straighter. He gets quiet. Once I turn the car off, John is instantly back into butler-mode.

"Please follow me, Megan. My home is down this back stairway," he says walking through the kitchen and to a door off the butler's pantry. "It's not much, but it's warm, cozy, and reminds me of my Daisy."

Ms. Amelia was correct. You wouldn't have known you were walking into a basement, except for going down the elaborately ornate stairway. It is clear that Daisy and Ms. Amelia had thoroughly enjoyed designing this estate together.

"John! Wow! I can see why you would not want to leave here! Your home is so cozy and beautiful! You both did a lovely job. It all looks incredible!"

John smiles, standing a little straighter. "Thank you so much for your lovely words, Megan. I am quite touched. Indeed, Daisy did a wonderful job in keeping with the design of the rest of the home, but she added bits and bobs, paintings, and sculptures from our trips to Europe to make us feel at home."

I could feel John's enduring love and respect for Daisy, even after she had passed.

"I've tried so hard to keep her memory alive by keeping everything just the way she and I set it up back when we moved in."

I snap out of my own thoughts, as I hear John's words reminiscing over a picture he is looking at. "We were inseparable, a team, and I always wanted to please her and see that she was happy. Happiness goes both ways, but it sure makes life easier when you are both on the same page. In a partnership bot individuals must be happy with themself and share their happiness with the other. Oh sure, we had a quarrel or two, we are human after all, and what couple doesn't? We saw our life as a partnership and always looked out for each other. I loved Daisy, I would've given my life for her. The only thing I couldn't protect her from was..." His voice trails off as a few tears trickle down his cheeks.

I know what he is referring to, and if that wreck had not happened all those years ago, his sweet Daisy would be here today. There's so much love in his eyes for Daisy, that his eyes are sparkling even more! I make my mind up, right then and there, to never settle for anything less than a love like John gave to Daisy.

Giving his arm a comforting squeeze, I inform him of what needs to be done in his space before we show the estate. "John, please don't trouble yourself with packing very much. I want you to feel at home here during all of this. Just put away your family photos and those couple of pictures over there. After that, your area will be ready for tours!"

"Okay, Megan, thank you so much. And, if you don't mind, I do want to go to bed quite early tonight. The showings aren't starting tomorrow, are they?"

"Me too, John; I understand. This whole week has been exhausting in so many ways. If you can see me out, I will head for home. And, heavens, no! It'll probably be next week before I can even list the house."

John escorts me back up the staircase, through the kitchen, and locks the front door behind me.

༄༄༄༄

A few months later, I'm sitting in Oswald's coffee shop running through all the recent happenings and reading the local newspaper. Who knew I would have been solving mysteries and selling houses all at the same time?! It sure feels good to have the drama behind me, though, so I can relax and enjoy my work and my home. Sitting in an oversized armchair that is beyond comfy and bathed in light streaming through the window, I look over at the shop across the street adorned with pumpkins and fall decorations. The air is cool and crisp, and the warm sun kisses the leaves on the trees as they change into their rich hues of golds, reds, and auburns. What a fitting time of year for us all. Just as Mother Nature prepares herself for winter and the temperature drops, so, too, the town is letting old things fall away in preparation for the new that is to come. Just around the corner is Halloween, a time for shadows, creepy ghost stories, and all things dark.

Shadows. Ms. Amelia has had her fair share of shadows

following her for way too many years. The ghosts of her past she could never escape from, both literally and figuratively. The darkness threatened and tormented her. Her mind played tricks on her and the fear of being watched or followed was constant. Yes, fall is a fitting season for the state of our town of Alton Rose right now, for when Ms. Amelia returns, it will be like spring. The old will have melted away, and in its place, a new fondness for Ms. Amelia will emerge. At least I sincerely hope so… she has already suffered long enough in this town.

I sip my coffee and let its heavenly aroma awaken my senses as I plan my day. I feel a comforting peace knowing that everything will turn out just fine. If the last several months have taught me anything, it is to expect the unexpected. Grabbing my phone, I go to text Mona to see if she'd like me to bring her a bagel and chi tea, when my chair is bumped from behind. I'm sure it was an accident, given the unusual busy-ness of the coffee shop today, yet I still turn toward the direction of the bump, only to see a lavishly dressed Ms. Amelia, leaving the coffee shop! She opens the door then mouths the words, "Check your pocket," while waving good-bye. My eye's follow her to a car with John at the wheel. *Oh, that's right! Today is the day Ms. Amelia is flying away on her vacation.*

I reach into my pocket with great curiosity. Pulling the folded paper from my pocket, I see it's bright violet in color with flowers printed down the side, such a stark contrast from all the other white cardstock she'd typed her previous messages on. I unfold the paper and read her handwritten note. Chills run down my spine. She did WHAT?

Epilogue

As time moved on, I began feeling calmer and lighter, relieved and grateful that life granted me a peaceful existence. London confidently saw to the release of Ms. Amelia, determining that life for her would be safe during the course of the new trial. He, her attorney, and the judge even said she could take her long-awaited and much needed-vacation. Anita remained in jail until further notice awaiting her trial. And, as you'd expect, it didn't take long for new rumors to begin circulating that Anita had had it in for Ms. Amelia all those years and that Anita's true colors were now shining through. Maybe these weren't rumors after all, but the town and coffee shop had been buzzing with talk of the case.

Woven within the gossip, it seems there is a renewed sense of respect for Ms. Amelia. She had, in all fairness, been through a lot. Her ex-husband, Hunter, was still awaiting trial for trespassing, accomplice to a crime, and knowingly selling a stolen painting. London, Gabe, and the District Attorney took their time coming to an agreement as to what charges to book John's twin with, as he played a significant role in conspiring against Ms. Amelia.

It took another couple of months for jury members to be picked in the new trial. Finally, the court began its prosecution against Anita. During all of this, I managed to sell the estate, but it certainly wasn't in the traditional manner by any means.

In the middle of the chaos and stress of court interviews, Ms. Amelia had still insisted on having a final party in the house for her children and their families. She expected me to help her and John plan the weekend, as well as see to it that each of her children had the items from their rooms. Business had picked up, as word had gotten around about the mystery-solving realtor. I was forced to juggle many different hats, all while staying up to date with my other clients and court interviews of my own.

After all the work Mona and I had done, and all the showings the estate had, it still turned out to be a private sale. And, although I never met the man in person, Ms. Amelia said it was an old family friend whom she's known and trusted for years. At her insistence, she'd paid me handsomely, giving me what would have been my commission and then some. She cited all the extra work I had done for her and that she wanted to show her profound gratitude for going above and beyond. Since the housing market is full of surprises, I didn't feel I could enjoy my commission check from the sale of the estate. Rather, I tucked it away for the unexpected - a rainy day as you will.

After a hair-raising and emotionally charged few months of more questioning, interviews, and long court days, many of which I was grateful to be excused from, all charges against Ms. Amelia in the original case were dropped. The town had been so on edge and hateful, London saw it necessary to publicly absolve her. Doing this did help ease much of the town's hostility against her, but there will always be the people who continue to choose to believe a lie even when faced with the truth.

It's funny how life takes you on journeys you never would've expected to go on, or forces you out of your comfort zone. My life sure has. I've now begun looking forward to the unexpected. I've come to expect almost nightly calls from Ms. Amelia, as these began when she set out on her first - and very lavish - vacation as a free woman. She felt the need to give me a rundown of each day. I'm so glad she is happily loving her newfound freedom and traveling the world. It's crazy to think she will still be out traveling for another few months! I've settled into my new home, but still can't believe how everything has turned out. London and his team are making great headway in wrapping up the new cases. Yes. I'm grateful things are looking up for everyone I know and love.

As I take in another gorgeous sunset, I wonder what life will hand me next.

About The Author

Sarah Mae Phipps

Up and coming best-selling author Sarah Mae Phipps is the author of a two-book series, If Walls Could Talk: The Mystery of Alton Rose.

Her love of writing began in elementary school where she received many Young Author Awards. After receiving her degrees from Mount Vernon Nazarene University and a Masters of Christian Education from Nazarene Theological Seminary, a series of unfortunate events pushed her dream of becoming a published author into the center of her world. Not knowing the meaning of the phrase: you can't do that; she vowed to tell this person's story in a creative way, no matter what.

With a crazy story of her own, this Hoosier born native and singer is a lover of coffee, naps, the English Countryside, and long walks in nature.

Publishing

Your Compass Within Publishing was founded by Kristen Franey in 2021 to give voice to women's stories. As an independent publisher, Kristen works closely with her authors to share stories of deep transformation so that their stories may inspire others. Together we also work to give back to the communities that support and nourish us. You may contact Kristen at info@yourcompasswithin.co

Printed in Great Britain
by Amazon